MW00679399

Scarlett

Holmes

Sister of Sherlock

Contrarian

L Charles Stribling

Paperback ISBN 978-1-80424-036-6
ePub ISBN 978-1-80424-037-3
PDF ISBN 978-1-80424-038-0

Published by Orange Pip Books
335 Princess Park Manor, Royal Drive,
London, N11 3GX
www.orangepipbooks.com

Scarlett the Schoolgirl

Let me, John Watson, friend of Sherlock Holmes the renowned private detective, introduce you to his sister: Scarlett. From the day I met her she, was the apple of my desire and the cactus of my life - clever, attractive, prickly, fascinating, and uncatchable.

Look with me into the flowering of this femme fatale.

Spring had arrived in Baker Street. The sun had risen high enough at midday to send fresh light into our curtained rooms. For an hour I mused alone while the coal dust around the hearth sparkled, both on the tiles and in the air above them. Mrs Hudson would soon be changing the winter drapes - hanging those thin, flowered curtains she kept for summer. I was looking back through time.

The village where my people had lived for so long was celebrating the first of May. No doubt they would be watching the capers of the young folk on the village green.

It put me in mind of the story Scarlett had told me about her girlhood, when she had been crowned Queen of the May. That day had been her triumph. Other young girls wanted to be chosen, but she had beaten them all. It was she, who was being courted by all the boys of the village – or so she said. They were not of her own age of course, she kept her glances for the older ones – the sportsmen, the horsemen, those who were destined for the University. The younger fellows, she thought silly.

It had been strain. She could not slip and later have to confess to having been boastful. She determined to *be* the best, even among those queen cats who were a year older. She had felt lonely. Once again, it was her not being accepted by her peers. They could tell she was a year younger so, with smooth feline superiority, they arched their backs showed her their teeth. Scarlett just had to swim in this very deep pool and, gradually, came to beat them all.

The effort seemed to have marked her. She knew that, in her make-up, she had the power to attract and the wit to bamboozle but still there was, and is, her sensitivity to the wariness of others that hardens the carapace.

This short introduction might offer a light on the following tales of the barbed beauty that was Scarlett the Lady. I wrote these reminisces from my diary, noted, sometimes, as a salve when I had been nettled by her.

Scarlett & The Whim

Today, Scarlett was in a foul mood. She was at the front door and had demanded that I be brought down.

Up to that minute, I had been feeling cheerful. I was delighted to have the lovely lady make a surprise visit. The house was ready for a caller – tidy and shining.

I have to say that Mrs Hudson was an excellent housekeeper. Dinners were on time; visitors were shown in, and windows were so clean that the London soot had quite been removed. In the corridor, she had polished the aspidistra leaves and all of the brass, even the rattly round stair carpet rods. The lady was Scotch and practised economy with skill – carpets were turned each year and, *more* often, the stair runner was pulled up or down to move the worn part of the treads up to the riser. That was normal, of course; my mother used to have our maids do that. The carpet was thereby worn down evenly, in some houses quite a lot. It hardly noticed, even in good light, which is not a normality in stair corridors.

Yesterday had been spring cleaning day. Having been warned of that, I had spent the entire day at my surgery and Holmes had found a reason to visit Inspector Lestrade. When we returned that evening, pleased to find all in apple-pie order, Mrs

Hudson informed us, with some asperity, that Holmes's sister had arrived during lunch time. Not waiting to be announced, Scarlett had raced up the stairs. She said she wanted to catch him before he could escape her remonstrances. Holmes had gone.

Apparently, she had soon left, with a great deal of noise, but without telling our very correct housekeeper what she was about. It seems that when she had entered our rooms and found us both absent, she had raised her voice. Mrs Hudson had blushed to hear the words.

Today it rained, and Scarlett arrived with a scowl. She was a magnificent woman, but her ill temper was not something to be provoked. Here she stood, framed in the doorway with arms akimbo, and told me, after some pretence at apology for lashing my innocent *self* with her words, that on being in London and finding herself with an afternoon free because her dental appointment had been postponed in favour of someone in pain, and what is more, without due notice, a sudden notion had taken her – she had decided to visit her annoying brother. She told me, with little attempt at discretion, that she had wanted to set him straight on a number of matters of mutual disagreement.

As I have explained on several occasions in these narratives, Scarlett was a year or two older than Sherlock. When they were children, she had played the bossy sister, putting him through what she described as a corrective regime whilst he, a

6

small boy, had experienced what he described as bullying. She said it was a long time ago. He had not forgotten or forgiven her.

Anyway, finding neither him nor me, Scarlett was very annoyed, the abscessed tooth making it worse. As she left, she had stamped her foot on the stair. I have witnessed that sort of thing – a cart horse would be proud of it. Well, the thinned stair carpet under her heel had slipped down behind the loose stair rods, *all* of them. As she told it, the carpet was of lamentable quality. It unfooted her. With legs all a-tangle, Scarlett had bumped her way, step by step, on her bottom to *the* bottom.

Note: Stair carpets were full length and held back to the stair by loose brass rods in clips.

Scarlett & The Troth

Scarlett drew the curtains. I was to hide behind them. My back was onto chilly glass, and the draught of a partially open sash window sent an icy wind under my jacket. The window bay had heavy velvet curtains, which kept her secrets in the room, and me out. She had told me to be quiet because very particular ladies were arriving for a séance. I do wish the woman would tell me what she intends; I have been put into all sorts of tricky positions by her. Before she left me there, she told me to cock my revolver and listen for trouble. *Me*, a doctor, *I* was supposed to save lives? She presumed far too much on my army days.

With a slow sigh, I put an eye to the lap in the drapes. I saw little, the room was dim, my demanding hostess had turned down the gas lamps to leave only a rosy – should I say *ghostly* – glow.

Into this carpeted, curtained, rosy parlour, female friends materialised one by one. They seemed to radiate importance. Even among these soft shadows, they kept on their hats; each had a cloud of netting that masked their faces. The women each took a chair around one half of the circular table. Scarlett had arranged it so their backs were to me whilst she, central at the other side, presided much as a queen at her court.

They knew Scarlett, and each other, only by exchange of soubriquet. They had met by silent signal. Her friends, I had been told, were practitioners in the art of noesis – the phenomenology of perception, useful for those who operate darkly in the daylight. They called themselves Seekers. Today, they met as a soirée with the appearance of connecting with the future – tarot-time, if they were to be swooped on by constables of the Special Branch.

What they did not know was that the cards might uncover someone amongst them with a false *legend* – a contrived background. My lady was a spier on spies. That was why I, or rather my revolver, had been invited to this private room, as I later realised. Watching the rituals raised my heart rate.

By the left hand of each of them was a stub of wide white candle set on top of a tall brass candle stick. The scene was theatrical, magnificent. The women were duly impressed. They raised their heads and hats. Under the felt brims, their brows warmed. In the well at the top of these candles, in the liquid from burning, and next to the wick, Scarlett had lodged, unseen, a narrow nub of resin. Such could be obtained from Chinatown. In a minute, the yellowy flame would heat the resin and create a faint wreath of smoke that would wander by their nostrils.

The women sat statue-still and joined Scarlett in an ethereal hum a ritual to take them into a trance. The long low hum lasted two minutes and lifted them to a higher state. They breathed in the smoke. In flickering darkness, Scarlett slowly, silently, laid out cards with weird drawings: werewolves, wanderers, witches - creatures of the nether land. I watched, quite fascinated. The humming faded. Breathing became heavy as they entered a laboured trance, they had become the: Seekers.

On the table, the wavering light of the candles revealed the layout of the cards: a pattern of odd number rows signifying The Book of Troth. The cards took in the low light and seemed to return a greater glow. It insinuated that meaning, arising from their arrangement, into the women's now naked minds: A low, wavering, voice which must have been the Seer, seemed to rise from those potent cards:

'We are The Book of Troth. We are a deck of cards, each different, each the same. Each of us has a picture of deep meaning, from the Fool to the Devil, and from the Heavens to the Earth. Only the Seer can brush from us the dust of obscurity.

'The mystery in each picture, brings the mind of the Seeker to recollection, reflection and projection. We, the cards, lie under the eye of each Seeker, but the eyes of our painted faces peer backwards, as does the Devil, down and down through a dark chimney, into the earthy caverns of Purgatory. We are drawn from The Book of Troth. That stack of cards which has been stirred in the sight of the Seeker is the: Book. Each card is a page. The story is in the sequence. The Seer makes patterns of three or five or ten or fifteen. As more cards are laid, the Seeker sees more deeply into the tangles of truth – more than they wish perhaps. More than is good for them. More than is good for others.'

It was evident to me that the minds of these Seekers had had to be readied with a trance – the smoke and faint light from a tall, thin candlestick having a wick of only a single cotton thread. Behind my curtain, I was glad I was not in this séance, *but* I *was*. Gradually, through wide-open pupils, I could see the cards. In that moment, *I* could have read their message - I felt boundlessly wise. Some of the smoke had seeped into my own head so I could hear or feel or sense what they were telling us.

'Breath Seeker, breathe in the smoke and see into the depths.'

I also breathed; I could not avoid it. The warm air brought with it some of the sweet resinous vapour. In moments, my world had lifted. I was as if a bird, floating, looking down onto the table. I watched, fascinated. The play began. Each pattern was laid before each Seeker. All cards were laid face down; each was *kept* so until the pattern was complete.

The humming ceased when Scarlett – the Seer – raised her palm, hovering it. Majestically, she lowered it to the first pattern. She turned each row with an incantation whose ardour was owed to the Craft of the Dark. Each Seeker echoed that incantation in a gravelled voice. The cards seemed to speak again.

'Only those who believe will see, only those who believe will understand. Only those who believe will benefit.'

Was Scarlett murmuring with closed lips? The woman sometimes seemed to be the conduit of a distant source – how could she know; how could she perceive the truths that she did? My mind was being taken around the cliffs of the unknown. The low voice rumbled around the room. It was deep. With my eyes shut, I could imagine an organ in its lower register.

'The Seeker is the soul who truly, *truly* needs to see their future. The Seer is the one who has learned the Tarot from childhood through ritual and sacrifice. We, the cards, are as doors, or curtains or key holes.'

It was mesmerising – I and they, all, were carried along with the wraiths of mystery.

'Behind us is a sight of the future.'

The cards were inviting us to see into the future, the thing that all the philosophers and reached for. We were enthralled, captivated, controlled.

'The picture of the future is different for each Seeker on each day.'

We all wanted to see this vision, but we were held.

'It is painted as light on wisps of a mist that folds and moulds and merges one with another in the moving zephyrs of time. The vision grows in the minds of the Seeker and the Seer.

Both see only with the mind. We are us and we are you, but you have a dappled being.'

The words ceased, the women waited, and so did I.

Scarlett laid ten cards in the shape of an H, then swept her hand in a slow arc pointing to the sisters. She paused by each, one by one. Her finger was not hers. It rose like a branch blown in the wind from a wrinkled trunk whose roots grew from the cards. The pressure on the minds was intense, fierce, like a heated sabre cutting, severing, cauterising, until . . .

A screech rent the dark and a sister ran from the room. I burst out of the drapes and chased her. The door swung, and swung again, the draft in the hall passage chilled my blood. The garden door banged, I followed but I was losing her in the windstorm and the flinging, whipping branches of the garden. I returned to protect Scarlett from whatever might else might happen in that devilish séance, but the sisters had gone.

Alone at the table, she smiled her thanks and, as a reward, laid out the cards. I was not sure what I expected or what I understood.

Once more they glowed. 'We, the cards, bring to our Seer her powers of deep perception.'

I breathed hard, was this the source of noesis, her profound powers of perception? Did she connect with the supernatural?

She was intriguing, entwining, divine even. Could I be embraced in that piquant spiral? My heart was beating hard.

'Consulting the cards shows the chances of love, bravery or foolishness.' The murmur was indeed from Scarlet.

It was telling me something quite special, not a secret, not to me. My breath came quickly. My skin became tingly.

The card of love turned up. Oh! Oh, she had foreseen the requiting of my desire. I raised my eyebrows in question, in hope, in yearning, but she swept up the cards and smiled like the Mona Lisa – as passionate as paint.

Note: Victorian Tarot had different decks of 78 cards with significant pictures and other occult areas. Fifteen or nine or seven were laid in three unequal rows and a forecast read from the sequence and proximities.

Scarlett & Danger

Women choose a suitor from men who are brave. It is all rather primitive. We modest fellows tend to be forgotten. On a walk across a farm one day, I had a chance to win Scarlett's favour with an act of daring:

'Blood! Look. The door post is streaked with it.'

Scarlett pulled the door open, and a body leaned out of the darkness. There was no head; ligaments were torn, and drips of blood glistened from the severed arteries of a wrenched decapitation.

I had seen dismemberment when I soldiered in Afghanistan.

Here, this mutilated body was not alone; bodies were strewn – a theatre of terror. Blood streaks and strips of flesh led around the back. There would be others, their bodies also mutilated, horrible. It was early, we were out in the dawn. The sun was just glimmering above the hills. The killer might yet be here, sated with this grizzly work, but still able to inflict injury.

This was my chance to win the fair lady. Women cling to heroes, particularly those who quote poetry, or so I had been told. I drew breath.

'Wait here, pretty lady. *I* will deal with this.'

She clasped her hand over her mouth in horror. '*You*, John? *Do* be careful you could be hurt.'

My chest swelled up. I was the hero of the day. She had revealed hidden feelings for me – her feminine heart was aflutter at the danger I might be in. A soldier's dilemma arose: capture her affections this instant with a smothering of kisses, or, go and do my duty?

Her hand was still over her mouth, leaving me with the second, less desirable, option.

Seconds passed. Across my mind marched visions of chivalric tiltyards, with admiring ladies waving veils to their favourite knights. Flags and crowds and the thrill of danger...

'What are you going to do, John?'

I could embrace her and kiss her and feel her melt into....

'John! Are you going in there?'

Ah, missed a trick, I had to do the hero thing before the magnificent maiden would yield her reward. Silly me. Standing there was an amazon waiting with arms akimbo.

'Or shall *I* do it?'

She would too. The woman tucked her skirts up into her waistband and prepared to do battle. Time for me to retrieve the honour of my regiment - the Middlesex had a proud reputation.

I put a comforting arm around her shoulders. 'No need dear lady, I will deal with this savage.'

Scarlett was stiff, no doubt controlling her fear, or maybe it was her temper.

'Well?' This time her voice had an impatient edge. It was clear that I had to do something, *now*. Go into the attack. First, I gave her a quick squeeze – a soldiers' final farewell. Next, for the full heroic effect, I had to quote poetry:

'Once more unto the breach dear friends.'

Her eyebrows rose quite a lot and she still had her hands on her hips – a classical pose I suppose; there must be a Greek statue like that somewhere. She frowned. Quickly, I turned my attention to a tactical appraisal. My military training came flooding back – the officer's maxim – reconnaissance is seldom wasted.

Plan one (or was it two?) had to be re-appraised: despite my cunning pause, the malefactor had *not* run for the hills. Unfortunately, that narrowed the tactical options – it left *me* still to take on him *and* his weapons with just my bare hands. At this point, I became very conscious that my army service was as a medical officer, not an infantryman.

Scarlett took up a hay fork. No doubt she would have waved it like the women on the Paris barricades did against Napoleon's artillery pieces. History said *they* came to a sticky end. I had to save the women – this woman – from foolish bravery.

I steeled my resolve, drew a long breath and strode around to the back of the house. My fists were raised, and my tendons were taut. The gravel crunched as I shouted a terrifying war cry:

'Into the valley of death.'

Alas, I was not the Six Hundred Lancers, only the one, and no lance, but the noise had its affect.

Within the wooden house, there was a mighty scrabble followed by a squeal. A flurry of fur and teeth and claws.

Scarlett had pinioned the befeathered murdering fox by its own blood-spattered neck.

Note: Foxes usually rip the heads off chickens. They will kill as many birds as they can in a frenzy if they get into a coop.

Scarlett & The Fire

A clanging brass bell scattered the pedestrians as a pair of cantering greys hauled a steam pump along the road. Over the street from me, behind the upper windows of a dress shop, smoke billowed. The knights of the hose and their chargers, the fire brigade's stallions stamped to a halt, shoes sparking on the cobbles and nostrils blowing. The pumps had arrived. Six stout fellows in brass helmets leapt down. They were followed by another red carriage with straining horses.

At the first floor of the dress shop, glass was exploding in shards, descending as glittering daggers. Charred embers floated up like black butterflies. At the engine of the great brass water pump, a man shovelled coal into the roaring maw of the boiler furnace. Wisps of steam curled up from the heating boiler. Slowly, the flywheel began to turn – the pistons were driving in and out, pumping water from a nozzle. The London Fire Brigade had arrived.

No ladder men were to be seen, but the uninformed stalwarts unreeled hoses at the double. Noise, steam, smoke – it was 1812 all over again. The hand of Hell was here, but Satan was not sated.

Before my unbelieving eyes, an apparition appeared at the second-floor window. It resembled a tall woman in white. She spread her arms like an angel rising to Heaven. When they had heard the fire pump's bell, the fellows of my club had gathered with me at the front window. They saw and pointed. I saw *her* and shouted - It was frightening. They recognised her too.

'Scarlett!'

Was it her? It was, it was.

The words howled out of me; I was shaking. Unbeknownst to me, my dearest lady had been in the shop. Now, she was trapped. The flames roaring up from below were licking at the ceiling beneath her. They would soon collapse the floor she was standing on.

I had to save her.

I shouted: 'Don't pull up the sash.'

Could she have heard me? No, but it only needed a such a vent to draw the flames through the floorboards. I ran out of the bar and down the stairs. The thickly carpeted steps nearly had me sprawling. I burst out of the doors to run across the road. Outside, the bobbies had arrived, and in officious duty, tried to restrain me.

'I am a doctor.'

They let go.

But how to save her? There were no ladders and only one way in: that shattered glass front door. By now, the hose was pouring water right into the lower windows, onto the seat of the flames where an oil lamp had dropped. Clouds of vapour misted the shop. It was Hell – flames, fire, fog and falling timbers.

Madness took me. I lurched in front of the hose and stood there. In moments, my clothing was drenched and proof from flames. Then, I ran through that fiery door. Inside, I hit a searing wall of heat rising from floorboards. I bounded in long strides, as if flying. Splinters of living flame fell from the ceiling. My jacket, wet and hunched over my head, saved the red-black embers from scorching my face. I breathed in the blistering odours of Hell.

At the back of the shop, the stairs were starting to leak small flames. I ran up it to reach her, taking two or three steps at a time. In the corridor at the top, the green carpet runner was smouldering and smoking – a vilely contrasting to the red flames. Where to stand? Where to go? What to do? Push through the doors, the next flight up must be behind them. The other side had been protected and quiet, but opening it brought a rush of roasting air into it with me – and pain.

At the top, I ran this way and that – a panic of pain. There, I had found it, found the room where my Scarlett was in danger – soon she would be burned like a Christian martyr. The door yielded to my shoulder.

Scarlett stood icily spread against the cool of the window. She turned to greet her savour. 'John! What are you doing here? You have opened the doors and brought the fire to me.'

'I have come to rescue you.' I wheezed the words.

'Very brave John, but *foolish*. The professionals will bring a ladder. We cannot escape down the stairs.' Her calm logic.

'No ladders out there, and we can't risk the stairs. We must go, now, the floor could collapse.'

She blanched and put her head out to see the street.

'The roof, Scarlett, the roof.'

I snatched her arm. She pulled back. I hauled and she staggered – Scarlett was ever contrarian. There just had to be a stair to the roof, there was *always* a stair to the roof – I hoped.

At the top, we climbed out onto the tiles and clung to the brick chimney stacks while the fire below was washed away by those brave men. Scarlett was quite ashen as she clung to me. The moment was intense. She was feminine in her fear and saw in me the hero. She was delicious. It was ecstasy.

'You were so madly brave John. You ran into the fire when the firemen stayed outside. You risked your life. We both could have been burnt to cinders – such a roaring Hell. You are such a good man. I am so grateful; I am so lucky. Thank you for saving me, John.' Then she bent and gave me *one* chaste little peck on my cheek.

Scarlett & The Wound

The street rose up at me, then all was stars, and hard and painful.

'John, John, are you alright?'

'No, of course I am not.' Fatuous question: it hurt.

'Well, if you are going to be like that, I will leave you lying there. Have you been drinking?'

'No, of course not. My leg gave way, it's that infernal Jezail bullet.' I gathered my knees like a camel and held onto Scarlett's coat while I heaved myself up. My leg and head hurt. I clung on to her arm.

'You can't lean on me, you're covered in horse muck from the road. Just look at your chin, it's bleeding.'

'I can't look at my chin, woman, it's below my eyes. Just help me to the horse trough.'

Scarlett was not amused. 'I will push you in it.'

This boded ill for an harmonious future.

'Women are supposed to be comforting to a man, not contumacious.'

'I didn't ask to be a woman. You don't know how difficult it is.'

Ha! Protected and provided for, they are.

25

'Neither do you, you don't act like one. Not until you want something that is.'

She stretched tall for a moment and smiled, not at me, but rather at some inner vision – Salome, or Catherine perhaps, making use of a young officer. She bent her head down and looked at me from under her eyelids with that slight curve of the lips.

'And *then* you *give* it to me, don't you John.'

I sighed. I did, I doted on her. Women have such power.

We stumbled to the trough. Scarlett told the cart driver standing there that his horse had drunk enough. He was a mild man, faced by this termagant, he tugged the old gelding away.

'That chin will need a cold poultice.'

'Yes, I *do* know. I am a doctor.'

'Just now you are a patient, so *be* patient.' I groaned and hauled out a handkerchief for her to pad my stinging face. She clearly was *not* going to use *hers*; too small I supposed.

There was something comforting about her hand cupping my face, despite the stinging, as she wiped muck out of the cut.

For a moment, I was a schoolboy with matron. Matron liked small boys; she came to watch us swimming. Perhaps Scarlett would've liked to watch me swimming. Perhaps she would've liked to swim. Sea bathing had benefits, but a wet bathing smock clung to the body, and it was cold.

With these thoughts in mind, my graze began to feel better. Dear Scarlett. If only she could be with me always, ministering to me. Her face was concerned. Those eyes, *her* eyes, looked quite feminine. My hurts faded away as she wrung out the blood and soaked the cloth again in the water. This was close to bliss. Dear Scarlett, she was so close – I wanted her close to me.

My battle wounds had healed, though my leg was still weak; it could give way again. It had been a cause of my leaving the army. Arranging myself to lean on the granite at the end of the horse trough seemed the safest thing. Trying to stand on my own two feet held the risk of falling onto hers, which would spoil the hero picture. She stood in front of me, dabbing with her poultice. Scarlett was a tall woman; I always had to stretch my spine when she wore those heels of hers.

Scarlett brought her head close to see the cut. The *eau de parfum* she wore on her hair quite overwhelmed me. I could think of nothing but the heady, intoxicating scent of her attar of roses.

'We will have to close it. You don't want a scar; you are not a duellist. Let me press the poultice on it to stop the bleeding'.

I looked into her eyes and quite lost all thought except the pleasure of her breath warming my nose. She pressed the poultice as hard as for a horse – it stung. I didn't want to, but I began to retreat. As I bent back, she pressed home her attack, the length of her body quite coming to lean on mine.

My foot lost its grip and she followed me deep into the long slimy waters of the trough.

Note: In 1859, Samuel Gurney, MP and philanthropist, with Edward Wakefield, a barrister, started a fund to provide free troughs of clean drinking water for horses and cattle in London and other cities.

Scarlett & Her Love

Her glove now had a dark spot. The knuckle was damp – she had touched at the corner of her eye. She turned her head away, embarrassed or cross with herself. She raised the hand again, shielding my glance.

'John, you never *say* anything.'

What was I supposed to say? Was this an indication that my interest would be well received? For so long, I had courted Scarlett without any sign, any understanding of my feeling. I came when she called; I helped her when she needed it; I calmed her frustrations and I advised her. In spite of all, she had never responded to the longings of a man, this man, or *any* man that I ever saw. She was as haunting as a marble goddess, my Aphrodite. Since first I had floated on her smile, my very existence had come to depend upon it. I had needed it from that moment, I needed it now.

'*Dear* Scarlett.' My heart was in those words. What else was I to say? Should I declare my affection? Should I throw myself at the bars of iron that kept her from me? A bolder man could have done that; brutes with fists would have done that. Why did women go for brutes? A kind man would have worshipped her, be her servant in love, carried her into a perfumed Paradise.

Should I? Could I? If there were a sign, a clear sign, that was all I needed, just something that would assure me against that razor slash of rejection.

I looked at her, studied her face, wanted her so much. Had she given me a sign? Had she opened that garden gate? Was there to be a whirling dance with her? Sparkling light? I advanced, heart racing. Just one more sign, Scarlett, *please*.

'Dear Scarlett.'

'Oh, John, I feel so silly.' Here it was, she was reaching out to me – her scent filling me, fragrant, heady. I drew a breath to speak, my head said: *Tell her, speak, say it*. She opened those glistening lips. I leaned, I craned to catch the sweet dew of her words.

'There is a man.'

'What! A man? Who, for heaven's sake?'

Cold water drowned me. I fell, like a stone, down into the helpless, hopeless darkness: a well of despair. My chest thumped. My body shook. A *man*. Devil take him! She had spoken of *a* man, not *this* man – not *me*.

'We have been good friends, John, and I need your strong shoulder. Give me your advice.'

Advice. I would have advised that she pushed him into the bacon slicer. My jaw became as rigid as a hinged hammer clunking a cold bar of iron.

'Tell me what your problem is. I will try to help.'

I wanted to strangle the fellow! I would rip his intestines out. I would boil him in acid. I would stamp on his bones. Jealousy gripped me as if it were the tentacles of a giant octopus squeezing seething volcanic blood into my head. Jealous hatred was real and had the force of ten thousand tons of blasting powder.

Scarlett looked at me, suddenly puzzled. Her brow wrinkled and her eyes searched my face.

'What is it, John?'

'Oh, *reflux*, sorry. Tea shop biscuits don't agree with my digestion. You get this sudden burning in the throat. Sorry, too medical, sorry. Please go on. How can I help? You have a problem. Who is this man?'

A thought began to form in my mind: if I were to help, or seemed to help, Scarlett might *see* me, *think* better of me.

Another thought wormed through my mind: with Holmes's help, I might be able to introduce this fellow to the study of crime – close-up. Some of the criminal classes were able to dispose of difficulties quite quickly *and* permanently.

'Tell me, Scarlett, what can I do for you.'

Note: Poverty in the London slums bred crime, and thugs for hire. Those they didn't kill were often left badly beaten and permanently disfigured by sharpened belt buckles. Some gangs of 'stranglers' were banded together by perverse vows of loyalty.

Scarlett & The Creature

Scarlett opened the door with a haggard face.

'John, I have been having nightmares. You are a doctor. Can you help? It's awful.'

The lady wrapped her arms – but only about *herself*, I was sorry to say. Then, as she squeezed, she jerked and flung them wide. Her face was contorted. The nightmare had seized her again. I had seen such terror in an Afghan, stricken by the witchdoctor. She held her head and moaned.

'It slithers from the shadows, from a fold in the dark and rises, swaying like a cobra, but it is ribbed and luminescent pink. It has great hole in its face. Ugh! It has the face of a pig without eyes or ears – just a great snout with a jutting row of teeth. It sniffs at my writhing skin and twists around like the tentacles of a giant octopus to fill its gorging mouth. It wants to bite me, to drag out bloody lumps of flesh.

'John, in the night I flail my arms to beat it off, but they are leaden. I shout, but I am dumb. In the morning, my legs are all twisted up in the sheets, and slimy with perspiration. It's horrible, *horrible*. I have tried gin and I have tried laudanum – that just makes it worse. After that, I had visions of whole nests of them rising and wriggling, wilder than a willow in the wind. It makes me sick and . . . and the *other* thing.' Her cheeks greyed at the thought.

'What causes it, John? Could it be a curse? I had dismissed the stories, but here it is. John! I have dug into Egyptian graves and unwrapped sacred mummies. Oh, how I *wish* I had not.' She flopped, like a rag doll, all strength washed away.

Such a sorry sight: the duchess of all she surveyed, now reduced to a pale, trembling wreck. My heart went out to her, my queen, my Titania, the magnet of my desire. If my medical skills could help her, I could win her gratitude *and* her affection.

'My dearest lady, I can help you I am a doctor indeed.'

'Oh, John, thank you, I would be so grateful. You are the dearest man. You are my kindest, sweetest friend. If you could drive away these devils, I would be everlastingly grateful. Dear John, what can you do? I cannot speak of these things to others – only to you, in our close privacy.' She rested her hand on my arm and looked into my eyes with that genuine need, an emotion that I had only seen in my dreams. This was a touching moment. We would be close at last.

'It is, my dear lady, an inflammatory bowel disease. Nightmares often arise from food fatigue. Have you been eating heavy meals just before bedtime – too many pies perhaps? I know you are the special speaker at dinners. The tension while eating

34

before speaking can cause indigestion. Has your appetite increased lately?'

'It has. I feel famished all the time, but that part is alright.'

This was another indicator – doctors look for indicators.

Scarlett continued speaking, '. . . because I have been shedding pounds to get into some of my special dresses. I have been taking something. It is quite fashionable.' She puckered her lovely nose. 'A little tin of tiny seed things. One can eat and lose inches – they are wonderful. '

A particular diagnosis was indicated – it was clear.

'Scarlett my dear, let us talk quietly. Do not speak of this elsewhere. I can save you embarrassment *if* you will let me help you in the privacy of my surgery. Treatment for your wild nights will involve Senna pods and tweezers. In your digestive tract, you have a tape worm.'

Note: The pill had a tapeworm egg inside which consumed the nutrients in one's food, so starving the body to be slim.

Scarlett & The Tramp

On Tuesday, Scarlett returned my note – she was *not* going to meet me. She was going to a private meeting with an interesting fellow who had a bowler hat and a red scarf and wished to pursue a cause. It seemed to me that he must be from a political madhouse. Maybe it was Bedlam itself. People there assume the personae of extraordinary characters but are often quite charming in their assumed role.

I set out to protect her, to accompany her if she insisted on walking to some dubious place. I started by calling at her club. It took some persuasion to have them to let in a man without a prior invitation. I told them I am a doctor, and that I had called to treat a woman member.

'I hope they kept you out?'

'They did. I tried showing them my Laennec stethoscope. I told them I was going to put my ear to your lungs. They told me to go away.

'John, I do have business of my own and it is *not* your business.'

'At last, I spotted you, wearing a fox fur stole, in a street, close to the back entrance of the Tsar's embassy. It seemed you were waiting for a man, or was it to be *any* man? What was the purpose of such a tryst, Scarlett?

'That is none of your business John,'

'Oh! Dear lady. Women are so tantalising. You were dressed to ensnare – such finery. You do not wear that fur for me. Scarlett. I was quite entranced, unable to control the fire you have set in my heart. Scarlett, I have to say it: I am jealous.' I took a breath and looked down. 'You walked away when I approached. I followed you along alleys and through alleys and mews, but you would not stop or turn - you just ignored me.'

'John, you could have ruined the diversion I was on. I told you I was on personal, private business. The appearance of *me* soliciting outside the Tsar's embassy was at Mycroft's request – it was to be a distraction. In fact, I was in drab, back at the servant's stairs. I was passing a pouch to the Tsar's attaché; he was to be recognised in black bowler and red scarf.'

'You have confused me Scarlett, but how brave, how bold, how beautiful.'

'You followed my brother Sherlock; he has the family features you saw and adopted my and gait. He was in disguise.'

Note: Holmes would have made an actor, and a rare one. His expression, his manner, his very soul seemed to vary with every fresh part that he assumed.

Scarlett & The Hollow

We had taken sandwiches wrapped in greaseproof paper tied up with string. We swung them from our fingers like children, as we wandered beside a rickety old post and rail fence along the crest of a field. The cows down the slope were unconcerned. A steam engine whistle echoed in the far valley, yet to pass the field below us. Its breathy note brought me the same little zest as I had had when I had admired this country idyl from that train track. Today, the pale sky wrapped this view in what was a scenic poem, guiding us to a copse of trees. I had planned it to be our picnic rest, and a little later: an intimate nest.

There we would sit and absorb the earthy air, a man and a woman together in a cool glade. The sun had blessed the day with a perfect afternoon – warm with puffs of pearly clouds that followed each other like sheep across the sky. Scarlett was content to walk quietly beside me, her arm in mine as I regaled her with my army adventures. Never was an afternoon more congenial. I wanted to kiss her.

We came upon that friendly gathering of old trees as if by happy chance. Ever inquisitive, my Titania hummed happily and detached herself to explore the wood. Her broad hat and loose blouse flopped as she stepped over the roots and between the brambles - deeper into the dappled shadows. She paused – as a cat might pause, stalking prey – then she beckoned me.

'Look, John! We could sit there, in that hollow under the leaves, and drink-in at the view – it will be cosy.'

It was not just a country walk; she spoke of it as in a midsummer's dream - an earthly lovers' paradise. My thoughts throbbed - my diffident courtship had succeeded – she was open to my ardour.

Scarlett was going to melt for me in the romantic rusticity of an enchanted wood. We stepped between the trunks into the shade of the great branches that reached above us. We found our glade, pretty with the pastels of fungi, moss and ferns. We knelt; first facing, then turning, to press shoulders, we settled down like fawns. Young deer might have rubbed noses in this hollow – their first tentative touch.

Leaves above us rustled in the breeze, blobs of sunlight whirled around us like dancing sprites. We spoke in whispers so as not to frighten the tiny creatures whose home we were visiting. As we sat in intimate silence. In a minute ants and beetles came to say good day. Perhaps the eye of a vole peered at us.
Here was a Lilliputian world of little creatures and little plants. We had to behave quietly, decorously, we were their guests.

We sat close together in an eloquent hush for some time, thought fading as we breathed the pungent air, becoming forest beings ourselves. The bed of brown leaves and fallen strips of bark invited us to lower ourselves down to the earth. Now was the moment for closeness, for intimacy, for two becoming one.

With a long slow breath, as Hercules himself might have done when he stiffened the sinews for a mighty task, I reached out my arm. My hand slipped around her body as dusk wraps the day. Gently, I pulled this daughter of Eve towards me. She yielded, then strengthened – surprised, I had to suppose. A turmoil of thoughts could be seen passing across her brow, then conclusion evident, she softened into a smile. Her shy actions would be my answer. I waited in happy anticipation.

My love reached down to a cluster of mushrooms on tall curvy stems, brown. She picked some.

'Try one of these. They have no white gills, so we can eat them raw.'

She, my Titania had offered me ambrosia. We would eat as if we were among the gods – it was ethereal. I stroked her fingers as I took the soft creamy stems and put them to my lips. Looking at her and breathing with her, I nibbled the cap; it was soft, slowly yielding, earthy. For a moment of perilous pleasure, I would risk all.

She returned my look, nibbled a small piece and chewed slowly in front of me, challenging me. Time had no meaning. I reached for more, and then more and ate them while drinking in her femininity. Like the gods, we were ascending to bliss.

I leaned back against the tree, I became the tree, absorbing the perfumed atmosphere through lulling lids. The bees buzzed between the buds and the drowsy afternoon settled into that darkish, purplish dimness, when the world wants to sleep. Time was as an old frayed string that has no tension, it lay in loops and was an illusion. My mind meandered. Visions floated.

Around us great tree roots curved up where the soil had seeped away with the rain. They were as the knuckles of giant fists gripping the ground. The effect was oddly menacing – as though some mythical giants had captured us. My thoughts wandered into tightening tangles.

'Scarlett are you happy here?'

Her responding look was questioning. I could be alluding to several different meanings, or she could be between several different thoughts – the female mind has many subtleties. Unusual ideas flitted in her brow, as butterflies do in a garden.

'It is the sort of place that forest folktales tell of goblins cavorting and playing wicked tricks.'

'Why? What are you seeing?'

Her form became wobbly to my eyes. Her colouring changing, her size varying, and her body lifting above the grass. I began to voice the thoughts hovering in my head.

'Look, do you see the shadows moving, do you see pointed hats and long fingers? There are long ears, with lobes like clock weights. Goblins have long ears, Scarlett. Goblins can set the carnivores on to us: black cats and foul dogs. Snakes can rise from the roots and mangle us in their coils. Whole swarms of spiders can march on us. Oh, I really feel rather odd.'

The world was turning in loops. Time was stretching and threading the clouds into silken skeins. Infinity was within me. End had faded into endless. Colours folded into a whirl of grey.

Words sank through me and slowly lost their meaning. I eased my bones, nudging some sticks and leggy little creatures, to crawl away. I was lying and smiling and lost to eternity.

'You have had too many mushrooms, John.'

My head nodded.

'Come along, time to go home.' Her voice was mellow, mesmeric, on her face was a smile, or was it a pretty smirk?

Standing straight, I reached for her arm. Twilight was descending as we meandered to the station. I followed wayward thoughts around my head, quite muddled about how it was that my plans for kissing Scarlett that idyllic afternoon had rambled away.

Note: Psilocybin fungi are the "true" magic mushrooms. They cause hallucinations because they contain the psychotropic compounds: amines psilocybin and psilocin.

Scarlett & The Place

Scarlett crouched behind a tomb. *I* was behind a stone monument, watching. Two days previously, grave diggers had quailed there and run. The railway company had called upon the council, who had shivered and called for a historian to investigate. Someone who could deal with horrors from the past - an archaeologist with a yen for the darker side of affairs. Scarlett responded, so much for *her*, as for me, as usual I had been called to help; my old army revolver might have been the reason.

The reason for it all? The railway was coming, and it had to have its terminus right in the middle of the metropolis; the very dignity of the thing demanded it. They needed the land, *this* land, even if it was a graveyard. The tracks were advancing towards it, like a giant anaconda, crushing the mean little houses in its way.

Coffins had to be dug out and carried away, but this forgotten field would not see the rails arrive until the ecclesiastical purse that owned it was comfortably filled. Until then, their reverences would have the Spirit guard this holy ground. It had been a holy place since shortly after the crucifixion. Poor parishioners gathered at the gates of their cemetery and prayed that this consecrated ground would be left to them, to be *their* holy help.

Their urgings for intercession had emerged in spectral form during the recent, sulphurously dark, winter afternoons. When the exhumers had cut into this holy ground; ghouls, those feeders upon the dead, were heard to wail from the graves. Those simple men trembled and glanced about them. They saw headstones move - rocking or leaning when approached. Bats dived, rats scuttled, and cats hissed, but worse were the ghouls: black shapes in human form rose from behind sacred stones. Paganism had not been vanquished, only hidden by Christian ceremonies. It spoke now as from a writhing pit of snakes. Stark staring fright had driven the simpletons away. Well and good for the poor folk, but the railway still had to had to have its terminus, here.

Despite witnessing the dread carnage of battle, an evening in a graveyard was not something I relished. Scarlett, the archaeologist, had accepted a commission to find mortal reasons for this immortal activity. As usual, medical need was her reason for bringing me. No doubt my revolver was also a reason.

We crept along inside the grimy brick wall and pointed a gang of men – idlers whom we had paid with an alarming quantity of beer – to march, or stagger, to where graves had been left open. They found spades and shovels, strewn about when the howling started. This gang of inebriates was less boisterous when they stood in the shadows of trees that creaked like crying children - bark rubbing on bark. They had been paid to dig down to a coffin.

Would the ghouls appear? Would the arrival of grave diggers conjure up dark spirits? We had gathered these derelicts one by one from benches outside dingy pubs so, loose limbed, they straggled up to one of the graves. On our sign, they reached down to the spades left lying there. Some merely fell head down into the weeds and spewed. Those who managed to pick up a spade shushed those who had fallen, then leaned on the shafts to steady their spinning heads. Their spades sank into soft soil – newly dug. The work was easy. Some of the drunks took courage and drove again. The coffin would only be a man's height down.

We peered into the gas lit shadows of trees that seemed to walk behind and between the gravestones. The unsteady men cast wavering, wandering profiles among the tall grey stones that leaned like the drunks themselves. We were looking for wraiths: yellow eyes and sweeping finger claws. So far, all was tranquil, just the whispering of curses and the slight screeching of steel on flints. The bell in the church tower tolled and the chill wind ruffled our coats. They dug deeper. This was a God-awful place.

Scarlett shuddered and looked back at me. I lifted my fob watch; we had been there for an hour, quite long enough. The mission was a failure. We had not scared up the ghouls. Nobody was there to frighten the navvies and be arrested – at least not this night. Scarlett would dish out coins to these degenerates and dismiss them. She rose, in her black cape, up from behind the tomb and called to the men in a chilled voice - low and wavering.

They shrieked and threw down their spades. In doing so, they cut a black trip-thread. The granite dais at the foot of the grave exploded with a yellow flash and a bang that should have wakened all the dead. We had stumbled on a new burial. It had been protected from the Burkers, and the exhumers, with a powder charge – a grave gun.

Note: Some mourners used to set up a trip-gun to deter grave robbers from fresh corpses. Burkers was the term given to grave robbers following the exploits of Burke and Hare in Edinburgh.

Scarlett & Boredom

Holmes was rolling his head against the wall. He seemed to crave something from the grey flock paper that decorated our sitting room. A moment later, he leaned back and pressed his fingers to his temples.

'Holmes do not bang your head. As your medical advisor, I cannot recommend such a thing. Please come here and take to your armchair again.'

'Boredom is *agony,* Watson. There is n*othing* happening, nothing to exercise my mind. I need work.'

Staring at the wallpaper pattern, because of having nothing to do, had driven the man to despair. The pattern would become very boring if looked at endlessly. The paper had a motif that repeated ad nauseam – Holmes need a conclusion. Wherever one followed the pattern, it was the same as where one started.

Holmes needed a tractable problem, something to engage his considerable mental powers. Without that we would both submerge under his miserable mutterings. Worse, he might take to strangling his violin. My mind sympathised with the man's lassitude. I had had such doldrums after my wound.

His sister thought such moods to be a weakness – by lofty contrast, *she* always kept something interesting to do. This had been put to me, with some force, by her on several occasions.

Whenever she arrived at our rendezvous rather *later* than she had proposed, she spoke of solving items on a problem list. Upon reading my flat expression, the lady would excuse herself by telling me that I could usefully have engaged the time, she had thereby given me, on 'spare problems'.

Waiting for a lady is something a gentleman was expected to do – without complaint, it seemed. Annoying, I called it. I had come to suspect that it was not mere inefficiency, it is a ploy to make her presence felt.

Sitting in an empty tea shop, as I often have, while the waitress scraped chairs and clattered cups, was an execrable experience – it was so vacant. Nothing had any importance, save the prospective arrival.

It was not that it was long, it is the unending uncertainty that was so dreary. There are no sensations, nothing to seize on - my head had no more activity in it than a clump of cloth. Time stretched, thinner and thinner, like a wire that might soon snap; much as might my sanity, or my temper. Extended frustration decayed into ennui, then into rigor mortis, and finally, petrification.

When I returned from my reverie, Holmes was still a prisoner of the wallpaper.

'Holmes, my friend, shall I invite Scarlett to visit you? She always starts your blood pumping.'

His sagging body was jerked in a spasm; arachnid fingers clutched then dragged as he tried to climb up the shear face of the flat grey wall. As heretofore indicated, Holmes and his sister were inimical, antagonistic, and enraging. He was escaping – up the wall as if he were trapped on the flat face of the Eiger.

Note: Quote from Sherlock: 'I was never a very sociable fellow, Watson, I was always rather fond of moping in my rooms and working out my own little methods of thought,' Sherlock said of his college career. Why did he describe those days as 'moping'? Because he was bored. He didn't mix with his fellow students because his interests and theirs weren't alike, and without that social element, boredom set in.

From The "Gloria Scott" by Dr Sir Arthur Conan Doyle.

Scarlett & The Punt

Bump! My hat slipped forward over my eyes to my nose.

The blunt front of the punt, pushing under the willow fronds, had scraped the bank, releasing that that sweet-sour smell of bruised grass. It is a scent that speaks of summer days.

Scarlett was levering the pole against the bottom of the river with her own bottom, and in bruised moment, had recollected a word from her classical education: 'Deodamnatus!'

It vented but did not relieve her bursting frustration. Her hissing remonstrance was not about the peril to my hat, but more about her not having shown the proficiency with a pole she had assumed she had when she insisted on taking over the navigation. A similar word had been uttered a few minutes earlier, when she felt the water running down her arm. That was when she had heaved the clumsy great pole up into the air so as to ram it, Boudica fashion, into the riverbed a yard or two ahead.

My gentle laughter at that minor misfortune had not been joined – a fellow should affect *not* to have noticed a lady's self-induced error. But then again, too stark an inattention could provoke vituperation about his lack of sympathy, gentility, utility, or any of one of the many spear-side inadequacies.

Our plan had been to slide along by the fields, embracing the upper reaches of the Cam, leaving the varsity spires dwindling in the distance as we searched for shade. The day was hot. Taking to the river had promised peace, quiet and a taste of that majestic wistfulness perfused from the dreams of the dons.

Punts are about as co-operative as the cows that we met on the bank. One could be forgiven for thinking that they had seen it all before and were dismayed at our spoiling of the greens they were going to eat for lunch. They stood there, guarding their meadow, silently widening their soft eyes at a lady forsaking her cushions to stand at the stern. Her long blue dress and broad straw hat had caught their gaze when she swished.

By contrast, they showed little concern for the fellow in the striped blazer kneeling by her feet. My trousers were absorbing the wet on the floorboards while I hauled at the string to raise our wine bottle suspended in the cool of the river.

As I mentioned, at the moment of landfall, my straw boater had travelled down my nose. It then fell into the water and bobbed away. Swift rescue was impossible because my hands at that moment were occupied with collecting Scarlett's wine. One hand at least, was needed to clutch at the gunwale to prevent an episode of involuntary swimming. My new yellow hat had thus slipped into the grey-green Limpopo and had come to resemble a fried egg, until it slowly but quite inexorably, submerged.

In that wink of a frog, I had had to decide which hand to use – still only having the possible use of only one of the two my mother had given me, the other was needed to hold me from tipping into the Postamois' realm.

There was a choice, of sorts: loose the bottle or lose the hat? To make that decision, there were considerations about each of the alternatives. Thinking did not really help, Scarlett was paramount, so I completed the task of retrieving the wine and merely hoped for the hat. My lady would surely have missed the wine more than my hat – and no doubt informed me of the fact.

I put the bottle in the prow of the punt, then I turned to the hat. It was visible still: the brim below the surface, but the crown buoyant yet on its pocket of warm air. Even so, it was sinking, half-pulled by straggly fingers of weed. Desperation! I had to restore my dignity lest Scarlett disdain me, so rare was such pastoral day in that lady's company.

I held onto the thwart with a Herculean grip, leaning right out to stretch my fingertips under the soggy lacework of straw. Despite arching my body with the elegance of a ballerina, my hold on the lacquered mahogany was slipping. A ripple from a vole lifted the brim to my reaching fingers so that I could begin to tickle it closer, pulling strands of the unwilling weeds with it.

A second dilemma was beginning to rotate in my mind: the hat or the thwart. It was as a gambler might choose which card to play: one seductive try to win, but in the very maw of catastrophe.

Time was enticing me, tangling the logic. I could do it, could I? One more second is all it would take. The hat was floating towards me, enough, just enough. The punt was tipping perilously under my extended weight. In a mere second, it would be nearer -enough for me to be able to scratch my finger on it.

Oh, merciful Fates, the calculation was paying off. I could save the day; all would be well. Scarlett could have her wine. The cows could have their grass and I could have the hat.

At that particular moment, Scarlett, dear Scarlett, stepped off the punt.

Note: From 1860, pleasure punts became popular on the Thames. It is a square-ended boat that has a flat bottom with no keel and is propelled against the riverbed by pushing with a long pole.
Postamois is a family of Greek river gods

Scarlett & Her Lost Love

Scarlett raised her hand again, shielding herself from my glance, then with a cough, she rummaged rapidly in her bag. An embroidered handkerchief flourished in the air – a distraction to disguise what she was doing.

'Excuse me a moment, John.' Her voice was quiet.

I laid my hand softly on her arm. She said nothing, only inclined to me – the tigress had shed a tear. My heart felt tight.

'Scarlett, my dear.'

'It's nothing.'

'My dear, you are distressed. Was it me? Have I upset you?'

'No, it's nothing.'

'Tell me.'

She turned to me. Her face had drawn down.

'Dear John. What must you think of me?'

She winced and heaved a sigh through clenched teeth.

'I don't know whether or not to tell you. You are such a close friend. I rely on you, you know that.'

Close friend? She had never let me near her, neither physically nor emotionally. I felt odd.

I sat silently for some moments, my hand still on her arm, but it had no feeling in it. My arm was rigid but trembling, not under my conscious control.

All I could think was that she had suffered a loss. Well, friend I was, admirer I was, yet hope did not die. I doted on her.

A glint of sunlight reflected from the silver milk jug and lent a glow to the porcelain that held the tea.

Could I help her? Would my friendship be of service? At least I could be close to her, but what would that mean? Loss of love was so blunt.

Sadness overwhelmed me too, but I was here, with her. I could help. My thinking was subdued and my words little above a whisper.

'What have you suffered my dear?'

She smiled, just a little. It was watery, thin like a poor man's gruel.

'Oh, John, have you loved? You share rooms with my emotionless brother who is so unfeeling. Do you not long for a lady?'

'Yes, dear Scarlett, but I do not know how to broach such things. They affect such distance, women. I do not know how to read the signs, if there are any. How is a man to know?'

Her forehead wrinkled. She puzzled at how clumsy men could be. To her, the passage of such thoughts was written on faces like pages of the Times.

'He left me, John. He betrayed me.' Scarlett dabbed her eye again. This time, she shone the full face of her feeling at me. Even I could see her hurt. This iceberg, this armoured she-tiger was showing her wound. That bitterness had an origin.

'He was a soldier – a lieutenant then – and he would have made a general, I am sure. He danced and sang. He talked brilliantly, and not about the army. He had studied the classics. We went to balls, and we were invited to soirées and weekends with some very distinguished guests. It is how I met some of the people behind the government.' She raised a hand to cover her lips. 'Oh! I should not speak of such things.'

There was pause while she composed herself. A sweet little snort cleared away the dross and she made to speak again.

'Often, we walked in the gardens after dinner. The scent of box rising from the parterre… He was a nephew of Lord Leicester. He left on a troop ship. I never saw him again.'

'How sad, I am so sorry for you. Do you keep up in contact with the family?' I was fishing of course.

Scarlett did not answer, not at first.

'He was a deceiver. I caught him with another. She was a cousin, another branch of the family. I had seen them together once before at these gatherings. But they were cousins, John. She was making eyes at other young men. She was such a flirt, so obvious, so shameless showing so much of herself. The silly fools, they fawned over her. I never dreamt... He was so affectionate to me.'

'Boys will be boys, Scarlett, and the ladies do take a fancy to bold men. For myself, I, …' She cut me off.

'But cousins, John. Such liaisons are forbidden, the results can be horrible. You know that.'

'I see it sometimes, in the workhouses; they come in from the villages, the sad wretches. The vicars should….'

'He recited poetry to me.'

'The ladies like that, I believe. Never had much time for it, myself. I prefer …'

She cocked her head away.

I had said the wrong thing. I had better learn some poetry, perhaps Tennyson? The Charge of the Light Brigade is stirring stuff.

Scarlett seemed lost in a reverie. I was lost in a mental muddle.

How to engage with her? A pleasant fellow does not cut much of a dash. Dancing was out; that bullet had seen to that. I could not waltz and even country dances were difficult, having to hold her with my arm up; some of these young women hang on a fellow's arm.

'That day I found out what scoundrels' men are!' She was almost shouting.

Several heads had turned towards us. I sat back and held up my hands against such vehemence. The turned heads did not trouble her. The hurt must be very deep.

'Not all men, Scarlett. Some…'

'Now I take my revenge, John.'

'Oh?'

'Now I give men pain.'

Her brother Sherlock would not have disagreed with that. His boyhood had had plenty – or so he told me. She had played school ma'ams once and applied the switch, then she threatened him with more if he said anything. It reminded me of the time matron had swiped at my bottom with a wet rag.

'There is no need of that, Scarlett, no need at all.' Nevertheless, I found the thought titillating. I shut my mind quickly, before I could become agitated. 'Scarlett would you like another scone?'

She looked at me for quite a long time.

Those eyes. If I were any judge, she looked right into me. Women had a way of reading a fellow that was quite uncanny, unnerving, undoing even. Tension passed through me. I drew a deep breath. Could I resist? Did I want to resist?

Scarlett & The Roses

Oh dear. The roses still had some drops of dew. It brought out the fragrance: heady, sweet, feminine. The spines were sharp; I had blood from several fingers collecting them. It was theft, I knew that, but there were plenty left. It did nothing for the pangs of guilt that squeezed me. It was hardly mollified by the plenitude, but who would not risk the park keeper's rage for Scarlett?

Did criminals enjoy the tang of wickedness that rises from the risk of being caught? I did not. Having done it, I had a battle in my head about whole enterprise.

Scarlett seemed to respond to rogues. At least that lost love of hers was one. I had always been the steady sort, not so charming. Alas. Clearly, I needed to have something bad to boast about.

The penny dreadfuls told of ladders set to upper windows in the fading glow of dusk, of nervous taps on the glass of a true love's window. This was always followed by the awkward emergence of a girl following a small suitcase. The whole thing ending at Gretna Green and passion in the heather. What they lived on after that was never explained.

My pocketknife had sawed at the rose stems. I could not grip them properly because of the talons that fought back at me. If I had not felt so frightful about it, I might had been more deft. As it was, I was a clumsy wreck. I dared not take my amputation saw. If a Peeler had apprehended me dodging about in the dark, he would have had me clapped in clink and the constabulary searching for a body. If they found corpse. Oh, heaven forfend! Even Sherlock could not have sprung me. His skills would have identified me – bloody gashes on my hands: a woman scratching her assailant. What was I doing?

Would Scarlett bring me a pie in prison with a file in it to hack open the bars?

Four stems and four blooms – red ones, not as large as they were. Shed petals on the soil testified to my clumsiness. What was worse: they showed the locus in quo. A cut stem or two would have gone unnoticed, but a spread of petals told of a crime.

No one came after me. The gate had not been locked and the rusty creek had not been heard. Sweat ran down my body from my armpits. Never, never would I do such a thing again.

I had to throw the wretched roses away lest someone saw me. Scarlett could stir a man to do desperate acts.

Scarlett & The Sewing

I had a need for a little help from a woman.

'Scarlett, are you sharp with a needle?

'I do not join my brother in that cocaine habit.'

'Heavens no, neither do I. It is just that my waistcoat is getting tight.'

She smiled at me and nodded. 'Ah, yes John, I would be pleased to help you.'

'Thank you. Shall I take it off now?'

'You might want to remove your clothing later, after we have conducted the proper ritual. Odin will need propitiation first.'

Did she mean the decanter on the sideboard?

'None of that please. I acknowledge only one God.

'Of course, and I will intercede with her for you.'

I felt that Scarlett was attesting to domestic skills – very comfortable in a wife. The future seemed to have roses around the door.

'Together, we will work a small miracle and make it fit you. There will be no charge.'

'Wonderful. Scarlett you are so skilful.'

'Well, it will take time – forty days to be exact.'

'Did your mother not teach her daughter to sew?'

'Revelations. Will help you John.'

Revealing my peccadillos would take some time, but well. 'Let me think: there was Mary, and then Rose and then Rosemary and then . . . .'

'John! I will mark your forehead with ash.'

Well, I suppose women do not like to have conquests paraded before them; even nobility prefer to keep them undercover, so to speak.

'Am I to be a penitent, marked with the tav cross?

'John, that would be the very End.'

'Oh sorry, I did not mean to distress you with levity.'

'If your Hebrew was as good as your Latin— No, better than your Latin, then you would understand my touch of humour. Tau is the last letter of the Hebrew alphabet. Alpha to Omega – the beginning to the end.'

'What? I beg your pardon, what did you say?'

My attention had been diverted to thoughts of Rosemary. If my regiment had—

'John, you are getting deaf as well as fat? I was talking about how the faithful could join the penitent – you – in study and repentance. It harks back to the period of introspection that our Lord spent in the Wilderness. You seem to be there already – or should be. Why do I waste my time on a man?

'I thought: 'Yes, it would be bound to be man I suppose, one who does not pay a woman of erudition the respect she deserves.'

'What in the name of Heaven are you making such a to-do about, Scarlett? All I asked for was a slight adjustment to my waistcoat.' I felt more than somewhat nettled. I could have done it myself. 'For two pins . . . If you cannot bend your mighty importance to helping a fellow with a little bit of needlework, well, I will just take a pair of scissors to the back of it.'

'John! You are a lump. I am doing that little bit of wheedle work. I will make your waistcoat fit.'

'This is Ash Wednesday - Lent will be your salvation. You have to fast for the forty days.'

Note: The Black Fast is a medieval religious fast meant to be practiced during Lent. It bars meat, alcohol, and dairy, and limits you to one meal a day, eaten after sundown. Odin is a Norse god of war. Tav is a last letter of the Hebrew alphabet.

Scarlett & The Orphans

Scarlett stirred her fork in the gravy around the meat.

'Apple so improves pork. Don't you agree, John?'

It was good – lean and tender. I hoped she would come again. Not often did Scarlett agree to join me at a restaurant. This occasion was only because she wanted me at her presentation of her research paper on immolation in ancient religions. Her conversation was sparkling that night – the food and wine had lifted her mood. I had ordered a second bottle and I could not now say which of my patients had told me about the place, or quite where it was, beyond the name: La Jeunesse.

She did join me again, and not long afterwards. Indeed, she insisted upon eating at the same place, so sweet was the roast we had enjoyed. It was a small establishment with a nondescript front door, off a side street in a part of London where the gas lamps were far apart. In the dark and the drifting fog, they were more like buoys at sea. The restaurant was only open in the evenings and specialized in pork dishes. My French was not enough for the hand-written menu but by mumbling and pointing, I managed to have the leering old waiter take our order. He said it was their *spécialité*.

The next day, I took Scarlett to the Archaeological Society, but she seethed at who would be allowed to speak. Of course, the gentlemen of that learned society required that *I* read the paper; their rules did not allow for bluestockings.

On the following morning, Scarlett arrived at Baker Street unannounced. Her brother hurried out – to catch a train, he said. She occupied her time with me on one of my visits to a boys' orphanage.

'What will be done with them, John?'

I saw that whole families were left in want when early death took poor parents. Here, huddled in a corner was such a family of eight, from babes to youngsters. These were lucky, if that can be said. They had no sores and had been fed – if only on vegetables.

I said: 'It might be possible to find a foster mother for these tender little fellows.'

She bent down to them.

'John, that stout little chap has amber coloured eyes. Look, the left one has a tinge of grey – how rare, oh, how endearing.'

We moved on down the room. I had others to see; there were so many orphans in London. My skills eased their sores and coughs, but I could do no more for them. I hoped those who were spared would learn a trade, but who would take them on, I had no idea. There were too many for the charities; perhaps they would do better working the land in the colonies.

On our second tryst, if I may call it that, we had to offer the cabman a little extra. He said the road was dangerous at night in that part of Victoria. Scarlett insisted and, once again, rhapsodised over the quality of the pork. I was afraid I had just pointed to the same item on the menu that we had so enjoyed previously. Scarlett ate with rather more gusto than one might expect from a lady, but she came from a merchant family – one has to make allowances. Some of them do well in the middling strata of life.

Over dinner, we discussed a case that her brother had left to her. She was to write a Green Paper on women who paid to send their accidental children for adoption so as to forget them. These foster mothers were commonly called baby farmers.

Some weeks later, it was she who was so concerned about the poor little chaps whom we had seen at the orphanage that, since she was down from her halls in Cambridge for a day or two, we visited them again. It was not my pro-bono day, so we asked the cabby to wait outside while we looked in for ten minutes.

The family was still there, of course. We saw six of them in the corner this time, including the greedy little one with the odd coloured eyes. Children do sometimes hide when they hear people of good class in the corridors. We left feeling we had been dutiful. We had seen that they all had been fed – potatoes I supposed; they filled poor people well.

'It is a pity the impoverished have more children than they can provide for. It condemns the little fellows to the parish.'

I could only nod, but then so many failed to thrive beyond infanthood.

A letter from her college summoned Scarlett to resume her lecturing at Newnham, so I did not see her for two months. When she returned, she asked once again to see how those orphans were getting on. I think she rather liked small boys; she said she could eat them – women say these things, it is a sign of great affection,

We went to that same restaurant; I could hardly keep her away. The same grisly *garçon* leered under straggly eyebrows and asked if we would like to sample pigs' eyes with the pork. He said they tasted like grapes. His Gallic ebullience overcame our hesitation and we each agreed to sample just one.

They came with the slices of pork on our two plates: one amber and one with a tinge of grey.

Note: Sir John Franklin's lost polar expedition in search of the North West Passage had another example of cannibalism out of desperation.

Scarlett & The Rules

Journeys to Cambridge with its university buildings were always a delight – especially when invited by my admirable lady. When I met her walking by the River Cam, she surprised me with another invitation.

'John, would you like to come along to my rooms this Friday night? I will be at my college, Newnham, and I would like you to come.'

My heartbeats all bumped together. Scarlett, that intensely fascinating creature of God's higher creation, had asked *me* to join her in a tryst. Ah, thoughts of beautiful blunders in dark corridors and warm door keys fumbled in clumsy fingers made delicious pictures. Did I hear right? Was it so? Oh joy!

The heated dreams of boyhood nights were becoming real. Here it was, at last, at last.

The thrill set my entire body tingling from my toes to the tips of my ears. In the folding of a moment I was transported, I was seeing myself in a perfumed paradise where all was sensation, where the chains of thought sagged low and the mind was lifted, drawn quite irresistibly into a lilac vortex. Brilliant butterfly wings brushed against me, tingling and teasing and multiplying the anticipation to an eruption of ecstasy.

'John? Did you hear me?

'Yes. Yes, of course. I was just wondering how that was to be accomplished? The ladies' college is locked at night.'

Did I really care how it was to be accomplished? Could wooden doors detain desire? I had seen the way to Elysium. Even Hercules would have attempted the labours of Theseus.

'John, are you with us? Will you be with us?'

Her call was like the sharp snap of an elasticated garment – of course I would be with us, in person as well as spirit – we would sample the delights.

I would have skip over the wall, I would tunnel under the bricks, I would don a disguise as a tradesman and hump a bag of tools through the gate… The thought of tools diverted my delirium to the practicalities of pragmatism – burglars' tools would be best.

'John! I need you. I want you to give me an opinion on the sherry we are to buy this year. We are not normally, well… We are not allowed visitors after nine, but my brother tells me you are something of an expert, so it will have to be surreptitious. Don't get caught.'

Oh my, were we to spend an evening getting delightfully sozzellled before we fall onto the sofa? It was worth the risk.

'I shall be pleased to sample your offering.'

'A number of Fellows have been invited to a little gathering to try it, too.'

Damn, damn, damnation; it was not to be a tryst. What a fool I was!

'They will be some of our doctorates.'

'Am I to be bored by a blue stockings and a dreary evening of dull dissertations?'

'Well, they will be bright young women: dressy, adventurous, very talkative and single, I am afraid.'

Note: Newnham was established in 1871 for women only and was intended to be friendly.

Scarlett & The Stranger

My dear lady was walking with me by the church.

'John, would you like to be burned?'

'What? No!'

'Would you like to be cremated?'

'Not yet.'

'Don't be silly. When you die, I mean. It is tidier. The church cemeteries are filling up.'

'Well, the cemetery companies are walling off large areas. One can buy a plot. I would prefer Highgate; there is a nice view from there. In any case, the bible says one should be buried – it's about resurrection, Dear.

'They only resurrect you if you are a bit common.'

'What? Common? Me? How? Who? When?'

'After twelve years, the grave diggers haul the common lot up and burn the coffins, bones and all. Ashes take less space. Then the others can use the plot.'

'How would I rise to Paradise if I were ashes?'

'Paradise is for the Elect, John – read all of the Bible.'

'I will be dammed if I want to be burned.'

'Either way, John, either way.'

'What would happen to my ashes?'

'They put them in an urn – you can take them home.'

'Which of my Holmes would get them?'

'Not Sherlock. He knocks out his pipe in an urn.'

At this point in our dreadful conversation, I began to wonder why Scarlett was so concerned for my future. Could it be that this wonderful lady was concerned for my afterlife? How thoughtful, how touching.

'It said in the paper that Shelly was consumed by fire on a beach in Italy.' She nodded. I warmed to my theme: 'His heart was saved and sent home to his wife. She was able to keep it, or him, by her for the rest of her life.'

'John, how romantic.'

At last, the lady was revealing that she had amorous thoughts about me. I was delighted and quite converted to the idea of cremation.

'Perhaps we could have a joint plot. That man Marx was interned alongside his wife in Highgate Cemetery.'

'I expect people take their dogs there for a, walk.'

'Well, if I go first, Scarlett, you might like to keep the urn until it is time for you to go to the plot.' This was getting quite exciting – we could be interned side by side. 'Perhaps we should choose our urns now?'

'John, until that day, one should put such an urn in a proper place. Not like the woman who, for years and years, kept her husband's urn by the fireplace, sitting on his chair. Ghoulish, I call that.'

'Did she marry again? I'm not sure that I would want to be in her trophy cabinet, or yours for that matter.'

Scarlett did not lack for glances; even ruffians would stop still, fixing goatish eyes on her. She lifted her nose, but I thought she gathered glances like scalps. She could reduce a man to ashes with a fiery snort and, in her fancy, pot them in an urn. That she normally handled me with verbal tongs was a warning. From trusted friend and admirer, I could very well have ended up in her curiosity cabinet – just one amongst the strangers.

Note: The first crematorium was opened in Kent in 1879. Marx was buried alongside his wife in 1883, but later reburied in a separate grave. The headstone was erected in 1955. The Elect are The Believers – Mathew, 20:16.

Scarlett & The Bumps

After an intriguing discussion with Holmes, I asked his sister to my consulting rooms.

'Scarlett, your brother and I were discussing women last evening.'

She gave me a disapproving look.

'He was dismissive of your qualities, I am afraid to say, but *I* believe you have a character that has developed strongly in so many areas,' I continued.

She nodded slightly, while searching for impropriety.

'Scarlett, as you know, I use palpation and touch-sensitivity in my diagnoses. Will you let me examine you to pin down your areas of skill?'

It did rather blurt out, but it had been on my mind all night and here she was beside me – I just had to ask her. I was itching to put my hands to use on her. I could not just reach out; she would not have understood.

'I must touch so I can tell him how prominent you are.'

'John, all this is very sudden.'

She had not rejected the idea, not yet. It gave me quite a thrill to think that the delightful lady would allow me to measure her shape. Turning towards her to enlarge on my thoughts, I raised my hands.

'I have been looking at your wonderful head.'

'John, not just here, what can you be thinking of?'

'You, I have been thinking about you. You have such wonderful qualities.'

'Well, if your need is so urgent…'

Such willingness to engage in tactile exploration was a new development. A girlish smile lifted the corners of her lips, and she fastened her eyes on mine. She was amused. I could not wait.

'This investigation will cost you lunch, John'.

'Lunch will have to wait, Scarlett.'

She shook her head at my impatience. The next hour saw us at the Empress restaurant. Oysters were in season. Scarlett liked oysters, and so a man who paid for them.

As we passed, the dining room tables were being laid with starched cloths and silverware. The ladies who circled and dined and held their *tête-à-tête* there would be well served. I was apprehensive.

My lady shrugged and slipped a coin to the matron on the desk then. With an exchange of glances, she led us along to the lounge and found a sofa in a corner hidden by the large chimney breast, where we would not be seen. Scarlett sat close to me, faced me, lowering her head, so I could reach out and touch her.

'May I run my fingers through your hair?

'What? No – the pins. I will pull them out for you.'

With a few deft movements, Scarlett had prepared herself for me.

'John, tell me what you want of me.'

I drew breath, my stomach was quivering at the prospect.

'Dear Scarlett, the head controls and reflects ability. Let me just run my fingers to feel how your bumps have developed. I have been reading the new science of phrenology.'

Note: The conjecture that exercise of the brain in certain regards would cause expansion, and thus bumps in the skull, was ridiculed. Expansion or contraction of use in some areas due to greater or lesser activity, e.g., in blind people or taxi drivers, has now been found to be true but is taken up by re-allocation of the dendrites, i.e., plasticity, within the skull without expanding it.

Scarlett & The Pill

On Monday, Scarlett arrived rather out of humour. She was seeking some medical help. At last I could earn a place with her.

'My brother Sherlock shrugged at me and slunk out; he is sulking again, somewhere.'

'He has a melancholy.'

'Idle and perverse, I call it.'

'Scarlett, you need relief. Your humour is choleric.'

'What!'

'Well, you are not phlegmatic or melancholic, are you? You have not the patience for either of those states, and sanguine applies to the optimistic and irresponsible. Let me think, er, you like Indian spices, don't you? And plenty of meat.'

'They ginger up my appetite. Listen, trying to talk to Sherlock gives me aches. No wonder I feel hot and weary. He makes me so.'

'It is quite clear that you are choleric'.

'Are you being deliberately disagreeable?'

'I think you would agree that your disposition is: ambitious, athletic...'

'Yes, I am.'

'And short-tempered.'

'I am *not* short tempered!'

'I advise bloodletting. Roll up your sleeve; let me find the right vein.'

'You are not going to stab me.'

'It won't hurt much.'

'No! Now I feel nauseous.'

'You have eaten too richly; you need to clear your insides.'

She looked down and held her stomach.

'I can't shift it, John.'

'For that, there is a specific.'

'Good. Better than bloodletting.'

'Not for the same.' I turned to my cabinet and pulled a small carton from the drawer. 'Try one of these, Scarlett – it stimulates internal movement, but you will need to react quickly. You had better borrow the chamber pot from Sherlock.'

She took one of the small green pellets and popped it into her mouth with a glass of the spirit from Ireland (I found it a little softer than the North British distillation). Pushing herself up from the chair, she took herself into her brother's bedroom.

I closed the sitting room door tightly and resumed reading my journal. There was an article about the benefits of Lent and the humble diet decreed by the church – no meat; one has to survive for forty days on vegetables. Notwithstanding, people had better health afterwards. Scarlett should have honoured the fast.

After some noise that I would not describe, she returned looking pale and strained but feeling better.

'You can take it again, Scarlett, it is everlasting. They are made of antimony and quite easy to swallow. Ask Mrs Hudson for a fork to retrieve it with, then wash it, so that if you have need, you can take it again.'

Note: The Everlasting Pill was very small and of made of antimony. Swallowing it would induce severe vomiting and diarrhoea, thus giving the body what they thought to be a healthy cleanse. Worse still though, the faeces would be sifted through to retrieve the pill, which was advertised as re-usable.

Scarlett & The Kiss

Courting Scarlett often felt hopeless – a man can only do so much. Yet there was always the tease, the tempt, the tice, the wisp of ecstasy. As a mirage draws the craving man, so it was with her – *and* she knew it.

As it was, I suspected she had several admirers. Fellows paid her compliments. They too were drawn in, but careful. Moths and candle flames came to mind, but as Erasmus had it: faint heart ne'r won fair lady. So, I trudged on.

Of course, one cannot ignore the beauty in the women about one – firstly, they resent it and secondly: if so minded, they can respond rather prettily. Even women remark upon other women. For myself. I was not totally unattractive to the ladies; I had received some discreet glances from time to time. Indeed, there were some very neat widows from the recent wars who needed a good fellow.

It occurred to me that a frontal assault on Scarlett's affections was like charging a castle – a more subtle tactic was needed; perhaps the sappers had a way of toppling the walls. To wit, I could make a show of scorning her. No, that would be to tip the seething cauldron over me. Oh no, her temper was too fierce to risk a tease. *Ah*, thought I to myself, *temper rises from passion, passion brooks no reluctance - a most powerful response, if I could precipitate it*. I could fire her up into boiling jealousy. Perhaps if I were to make a display of attending to one of her students, she might flare up and, what a delicious thought, *fight* for me.

It had come to be that the study of archaeology, being a new subject, attracted women – quite a number of them, bright, intent women, some rather attractive.

Scarlett was to give a lecture on archaeology, so she agreed that some words from me regarding the interpretation of ancient skeletons was enough to have me as a guest speaker. There would be pretty young women there, all agog for explanations from me – just right.

The university had the use of a small hall. When I arrived, at the front, near Scarlett's chair was a particularly attractive example of the species. Shy, but eager. Her reserve soon burst with giggles, and she swept very blue eyes at all the other girls – nudging and patting them, too.

I was at the side of the dais so did not receive her glance, but her avidity sent a tingle through me. When Scarlett entered, she bobbed up and introduced herself. This little wren had become quite agitated. *Intense,* I thought – she would not be overlooked.

My plan was to pay too much attention to this girl, making her a very obvious rival to Scarlett.

When the lecture was over, the students started crowding out. I detained the girl and made a show of offering a favour: she might have liked to extend her study of skeletons and join me examining a cadaver at the morgue. There was a well-appointed hotel nearby which served fruit cakes with dishes of China tea.

Scarlett saw and heard all of this and strode forward to intervene. My plan was working – my love was jealous. Scarlett was coming to stand between me and the pixie, but the frolicsome girl pushed me aside, turned to Scarlett and caught her by both arms so she could plant on her lips a great, greedy French kiss.

Note: Whilst Victorians disapproved of its public expression, such lust and love of all sorts carried on in secret.

Scarlett & The Earth

Slime dripped onto Scarlett's hair. Above us, like the roots of a forest, stalactites glistened in the light of our candle. In the clammy silence that sank us in sanctity, spiders scuttled, their many legs grasping flies from the musty air. Her cold fingers wrapped her hat closer to her head and she bent low over the dull brass plaque on the yet duller lead of the coffin. Dust rose in slow clouds; her breath was blowing away spiders' frass and shells of beetles long desiccated.

We were in a row of narrow vaults built under the cemetery to preserve the bones of the worthy dead. Outside, under the grass, the earth of the Earth was engulfing those who no longer walked in the day. Over time, their wooden coffins would rot and collapse under the weight above them. Worms, beetles and other crawling, gorging insects were taking the dust of death back to that of oblivion.

Our minds were heavy with the aura of death. Our belief in the inevitable passing of time was fading. The past had stopped. Here, in this dungeon, it was Purgatory. The air was thick with the silent screams of souls wanting, needing, to start their journey. If skeletons were going to rise, these were they. It was the weight of lead holding down the coffin lids. Their only escape was slowly to turn sour and become devilish: their form remaining as it was, but their substances becoming a grey mist.

Fear was in the land; because bodies from funeral were not always dead, not completely. Old men feared that an illness that might induce a heavy sleep showing only the faintest of breathing. It could deceive the impatient funeral director, or the careless or, *or,* the conniving. A person might come to be buried alive, then wake from that coma to see only the wooden lid of a coffin above their eyes. They would be trapped in their coffin, to suffocate in spiralling madness. In some coffins a cord was left by the hands so it could pull and sound a bell above the grave.

Victorians, those who could afford it, were not buried in the ground. They had their coffin placed on a shelf in a brick vault from which escape was possible

Scarlett had had an insight, her noesis had seen something partially existing and woken her. She wrapped a black cape around her night gown, ran to the cab rank in her dash to Baker Street. She had battered on Mrs Hudson's front door like Beelzebub's bitch, waking the neighbours as well. I had been dragged from the depths of my dreams to join her hurry to the burial grounds. She paid our reluctant cabby to drive his sweating horse right into the cemetery despite the chill wind blowing twigs from the trees like lonely bones seeking sanctuary. We arrived right up at the mausoleum.

94

She was anxious and barely articulate. Her concern: to be in time to rescue from a coffin, one who was not dead, not completely? We stumbled down the steps lighting our way with no more than a candle. Along the sides were the vaults, festooned with webs. The floor was marked with the excreta of rats. We slipped and bumped against the brickwork, grazing hands and driving who knows what filth and disease into the bloody scrapes in our skin. A woman might have woken in a coffin and need us.

Scarlett was frantic in her search for a coffin that she had seen in her mind. The vision that she saw when partial facts and surmises and probabilities align. According to her, it was like a force like a beam of sunlight that lit up a picture. This time she had seen a woman – it was as if her spirit had contacted her. She felt the most dreadful anxiety. She would not explain anymore to me, became sharp and shouty when I asked for whom we were searching.

If I had the name, I too could look at the plaques, but she was not able to shape breath into that word. She just ran jerking, jumping, gesturing while breathlessly peering at the engraved words. We sped from one vault to another, all in that chilly darkness, as she searched for the woman.

Suddenly Scarlett stumbled and lurched against a coffin.

'Sorry.'

I had to reach out an arm lest she fell into the faeces on the floor. The candle fell from her hand, leaving us in a changed light: black shadows leaned out from knobs and handles that now shone in their passing moment of reality. The grey dust on the lid took fire from the candle. A ripple of small dancing flames spread out from the effigy of a face chased into the lead. It was as a halo; it grew like the aura of a saint.

Scarlett smiled, but the light showed her as a grinning skull.

'Sorry to disturb you.' She patted the lid. Scarlett insisted on good manners even to the departed. The lid creaked.

At the head end of the coffin rose a pipe, a breathing pipe and on a frame, a bell. If a man had feared being undead, if the cadaver had been pronounced, boxed and prayed over while merely in a deep coma, he wanted to be able to call out. Coming out of the pipe was a flaxen cord, once white, now a line of dust and dull grey fibres. Years ago, the little clapper in the brass bell could have swung on its trunnions and might have pealed a small plaintive cling-clang. The pitch would have been tuned to a disharmony that would shiver through the air to alert those above to the distress of the one inside. It needed someone to be near.

As Scarlett pushed on the lid, it creaked again. The little bell clanged, quietly but without stopping *cling-clang, cling-clang.* It seemed that a cadaver could, would, raise the lid and the spirit would float up as it had when the soul had forsaken the flesh. Scarlett, froze.

'Here she is, John.' She was clawing at the sides of the coffin. 'Help me! There is someone alive in here. I saw her, I saw her.'

It was horrifying, I don't mind telling you. My hands shook, but as madmen had the strength of ten, so I had the sudden strength of Samson. I wrenched open the lid.

Out poured a stream of rats.

Note: From 1 million in 1802 by 1850, the population of London grew to 2.3 million. London graveyards ran out of space. In 1832, Parliament passed a bill asking for seven private cemeteries to be provided. Some had underground mausoleums for long-time internment of coffins.

Scarlett & Her Feather Boa

Scarlett was always elegant. Her style was often a well-cut suit finished with a feather boa. It emphasised its strict mistress: the jacket tailored to her figure and the dress – slim and long. Beneath the skirt, were black boots, like those of a stiff, stern soldier.

Contradicting the school aspect of the school mistress persona, was the boa – not the contrast, but the emphasis. It was as the intimation of an earthquake – for me the very ground would shake. The quake was not in her – the sundering of the senses was in me. A whisk of Scarlett's boa was as a torpid snake springing up: bare fangs and a freezing hiss.

Her choice of feathers rather depended on her mood. She had four forms: ostrich or turkey for flamboyant occasions and marabou or chandelle – so she told me – for more restrained states, perhaps when lecturing from one of her papers. She wanted men to see her as serious, without forgetting that she was a woman, and could wind them around her finger. The boa, and the scent of eau de cologne that filled her wake as she walked, was of a femme fatale: fascinating but feared.

The lady revelled in the effect she had on the poor fellows. Tall and swaying, much as a dragon might sway its long neck when stalking. A dragon would consume its victim with heat and flames, so would she. She was undeniable but unobtainable – an ecstasy of pain.

The women she eclipsed were themselves both admiring and fiery. They approached with lethal intent then wilted and fled. A shy fellow, she could rope a to her by looping the boa over him and hauling him in or, she could bind a bold one tight, trussing him with spidery threads spun from twirls of that same boa..

The scent she wore was from a tiny bottle, found only in Paris. The perfumier's creation was not unique, but when it had been on her smooth and delectable skin, and it had mixed with the scent of her, it would take a statue made of stone not to bend and bow in such a fragrant haze.

Gestures with the boa were overtures: running her fingers along it, spinning the end of it, nestling her chin into it, all the while keeping those greenish eyes drilling into a fellow with a seductive light which she dappled with subtle smiles and playful dips of those auburn eyebrows. Men would bargain their honour to live one more minute in Scarlett's aura.

I could not detach myself from her, no matter her indifference, her dismissals and her pretty, pearly, perfect, carnivorous teeth.

Note: From 1820, feather boas had the reputation of being elegant and bold. *Eau de Cologne* parfum was widely worn, having a sharp smell that protected the wearer from other odours.

Scarlett & The Mood

Academics retain their tenure by producing papers. Scarlett produced papers but struggled with their reading in men-only institutions. She often came for help in high dudgeon. This time I had been summoned to meet in her favourite tea shop.

'John, my scientific submission to the British Association has been postponed. Women are so disregarded in this primitive country. We are much better treated in France.'

'Yes, women are glorified in France. I was once taken to that red windmill place in Paris, it was wonderful. They were so pretty waving their ankles at us, they were delicious. They . . . '

'John! You don't understand. Women should be respected *and* allowed to vote. If women were in Parliament, there would be peace and plenty.'

'Women of status have been allowed to vote from . . . the first parliament, they have always put their case. Castilians for instance . . . .'

The poor woman became hysterical, spittle sprayed out.

'Grrrr! Not after 1832 – the law was changed.'

'Well, Scarlett, judging by *your* lack of self-control, it is not surprising.'

'Men are so stupid, like bellowing bulls – how can they understand the restrictions on women.'

She stamped her foot, swiped at the orchid in the silver plant pot on our table and became red in the face. In the next moment, she slumped back in her chair, panting and gripping her fists. Her rage had blown out and she sagged like a punctured balloon.

'Perhaps I should beckon the waitress for more tea. Tea is comforting my dear, it's the warmth.'

'Oh, what is the use?' Scarlett's arms hung down and she turned her head away. 'Why do I apply my talents? Oh, go on. John, tell that silly girl to bring more tea. Darjeeling, not that Gunpowder tea, I don't like green tea. I want it black this time. Scarlett's outburst was thankfully brief but ended with a curled lip.

When brought to normal behaviour, she might, dare I think it, make a striking doctor's wife. I was sure I could make her happy – with a houseful of children. She would be in full charge of the servants and directing the gardeners. What is more, as a pillar of the community – the doctor's wife – her energy would be well spent organising bazars to provide comforts for the poor.

'What happened to the tea? Am I to be deprived of that as well? Am I of no consequence at all?'

'Scarlett, dear lady, I am so sorry, I was lost in a pleasant reverie, I was musing on the delights and comforts of matrimony. Have you ever considered . . . ?'

'No! Men are stupid. Until I can be the householder, the banker and the boss, I will not endure such a state.'

'Do you want to end your days sitting in a little room by a few coals in a lonely grate, your whole existence passed over and forgotten?'

'I shall make myself rich and well regarded. Ha! Important men will seek me out and submit to me for the brilliance of my company.'

'Fortune is fickle Scarlett, do remember the Flowers, they Bloom in the Spring, tra la.'

Note: The line: The Flowers, they Bloom in the Spring, is from the Victorian operetta: Mikado by Gilbert and Sullivan. The sentiment is timeless.

Scarlett & The Bliss

Smoke rings rose on the languid air while the dark, musky-minty fragrance of patchouli oil pervaded the room. A note had reached me in my surgery that morning. It was from Scarlett of course; I recognised not only her curvaceous hand but the scented envelope. Within it was an address in Lambeth within walking distance of the Archbishop's Palace. My lady of magical mysteries had summoned me, so I went.

Arrival at what was a quite ordinary front door in a side street had me greeted by a bowing Sikh. He took me through what was an extensive if narrow house. We went along an unlit corridor heavy with embossed flock paper of a torrid red. The passageway passed several closed doors and turned two corners. As I burrowed on, I was impressed by the heavy, earthy scent in the air. It became more intense as I was led down a flight of stairs to a basement room. Upon a tinkle of bells, the door opened into a shaded Indian Paradise. I was led into a sultry sphere where walls and columns were tented with silken cloths hung in swags. Deep golds and browns and orange colours folded and pervaded. There were no windows, the only light was the soft flickering of oil wicks on beautiful beaten brass standards.

The object of my affections was upon a dais, dancing. Scarlett was framed by intricately carved dark wood panels. Wavering images of elephants and storks fell upon her. She was curving and flowing to the insistent rhythm of a sitar. Her hands and arms flowed like snakes – she was Durga waiting to ride her tiger. The drums throbbed and the drummers let their heads float in harmony. She saw me and smiled. My pulse quickened and fell into step with the beat: dumba, dumba, dumba.

The Sikh took me to a pile of cushions near a large smoky brass lamp and I sat cross-legged as I had in the jirgas on the frontier of Victoria's empire. The beat of the drums and the heavy, scented air quite lifted me, much as does a second glass of claret – I became part of it all. Warm zephyrs wafted me to Nirvana.

Fragrant tea arrived in a small dish – such grace, such courtesy. As I sat, entranced, another woman rose to dance, dressed in wisps of silk, some of it falling across her like green mist. There is much to take the eye with an Indian dance: feminine slow-swirling curves.

My love glided over to my spread of cushions and sat at my feet, removing my shoes, then my socks and then brushing them with her hair. Her soft cheeks wore a most gentle, deserving smile. An Englishman is utterly at the mercy of a submissive, adoring woman. Scarlett had had an epiphany; she had become a goddess of femininity.

Patchouli does wonders to lift a soul from sadness – Scarlett had found a cure for her moments of melancholy. It seemed the lady had absorbed much of this heavenly atmosphere from the oriental glass bong that heated aromatic herbs on the low tables in front of me.

The earthy aroma of patchouli, that ancient aphrodisiac, had brought my lady to me. Scarlett took the pipe into her mouth an inhaled. It came to me that it was disguising the smell of marijuana. All was tranquil and colourful and beautiful.

I reached out to embrace her. It broke my dream – I now lay bruised on the floor beside my own bed in my boring bedroom.

Note: Patchouli oil has an earthy aroma that masks the odour of marijuana. It increases libido. It was popular again amongst the young in the middle years of the last century.

Scarlett & The Pain

The femme fatale delights in luring men into places they should not be. Scarlett often played the temptress with me.

'Some men find certain forms of pain – if sharp, quick, and experienced in a perfumed room – to be a pleasure.' Scarlett's words uttered beneath lowered her eyebrows was looking at me in a very direct way, a light grin playing about her cheeks. 'Were you flogged at school, John?'

This particular subject, raised apropos of nothing, seemed to reveal a certain ardour of intent – ecstasy awaited. I hesitated.

She carried on: 'There are similarities, you know, between pain and pleasure. Some boys come to enjoy it.'

I wrinkled my brow *and* some of my hair. I stared at her, my thoughts in a turmoil. Did I imagine *her* fingers holding a cane? Would my buttocks be bared?

'There is a thrill, the building of tension, walking the corridors to the headmaster's study, then: sharp pain sensed as joy. Tension reversed in relief. You understand me, I think.' She leaned forward. 'Did you enjoy it John, that "pain which is desired" as the poet has it?'

The walls felt close. My mind clawed at the significance of these words. She was a woman who spoke to a purpose. What

111

purpose? Was she searching for some fetish, some secret of my bachelor existence or just something to toy with as girls do with dolls? I sat back in my chair, wanting it to swallow me.

She knew something and I had better come clean or there would be convoluted, complicated questions, thick with inuendo. This was and would be, could be, very uncomfortable.

'Are you?' I stared at her; indeed, I could not pull my eyes away. The thought fell like a boulder from a cliff. It rumbled and bounced heavily until it splashed into the sea' 'Er. Are … you… aware of Bartolini's restaurant?'

Scarlett shook her head slowly, with an intrigued look that culminated in a questioning glance. Oh dear, I had proper done it. How could I escape the bonds that she had reeled around me? I had to burrow my way out.

'That restaurant has a back room where members can exchange details of nether doings, or so one of my patients told me.' I had to state a source for this information, or she would conclude that I was a frequenter myself. 'Scarlett, I do not know where you are leading me on this highly irregular line of conversation, but I have heard about this, in the confidence of a consultation, of course.' I frowned to emphasise that she must not divulge the source. 'That patient had told me that he was beset by overwhelming urges of an… intimate nature.' I raised a spread of fingers like prison bars to contain the forthcoming information.

'Some members, those of the legal profession in particular, are prone to, shall we say, unusual activities. They have to listen to all sorts of base behaviour. It stirs unquenchable passions. In his case, I prescribed a strong laxative. He had already used an enema. I hoped the harsh medicine roaring through his intestines would flush away his unwanted arousal. I must have cured him because he did not come back.'

Scarlett gave me one of her enigmatic looks. Seeing that, it struck me, that she might have quite another reason for her curiosity. Maybe I could reverse this enquiry and make the lady uncomfortable instead.

'Some medicines have powerful side effects.' I lifted up the medical journal I had been studying. 'I read here that apothecaries used to sell liquorice to quell such inconvenient passions as spinsters were prone to.'

Scarlett nodded and spoke while rubbing her chin. 'Some just enjoy it, doctor.'

This conversation was becoming ever more intimate. She seemed to be drawing me in to something delicious, but dangerous, despite her beguiling tone. I stood up, walked to the window and pulled the curtains.

'The evening is growing darker.'

I meant it to be a hint, but she ignored my caution.

'Indeed, there are many practices of dubious morality going on, John. In places, let us say, where gas lighting has yet to illuminate.'

I had better advise her what her detective brother had told me: 'There are private societies in London whose members enjoy peculiar practices. They have become fruitful sources for those who would blackmail.' This was getting closer to the point, and to a particular kind of ungodliness. 'Serve them right. I suppose they have to pay handsomely, or they lose their public position.'

The coals slumped in the grate into a pit of glowing red

'Blackmail is not just for money, John. It can be a powerful way to obtain cooperation. Sometimes good men are so drawn in by their weaknesses, they don't realise what is happening to them. Some are forced to take up causes they would not have espoused.'

I understood: In her secret service work, she was both an intelligencer and a cunning operative – she was planning a foreign spy's entrapment.

Note: Endorphins that are released in painful experiences are often perceived as pleasurable. Bartolini's restaurant had a back room in which respected members of male society would drink and discuss what they had heard or suspected of fetishes in the hidden corners of colonies.

Scarlett & Her Bed

Despite its wealth of words, the variety of meanings in different contexts made my understanding of Scarlett's English perilous.

'John, would you like to share my bed?'

Scarlett was looking down at her fingers as they traced the petals of flowers on the page. Her book of exotic plants was fascinating – so many from so far away, but she said we could too grow them in an English garden.

We were spending a fragrant evening together on an ornate wrought iron bench, by the wall. A big book was king of the table in front of us. Half-sipped flutes of sparkling wine shaped slivery harmonies as the evening air wafted across them.

Our heads were immersed in the scent of the honeysuckle growing there. Dusk was descending and the perfume was heady. Some wayward sun beams still reached between the elms and played on the gable of the great house. The soft amber stone seemed to glow. If a lady had a romantic susceptibility, then this garden would be her Heaven.

After our diner, she had taken my arm so we could stroll together around the lawn. I led her to it through arches of vines. Luxuriant leaves hid tiny bunches of buds that would grow into white grapes. By and by, we found ourselves in this corner of the terrace, well out of view of the wide glass doors. Scarlett had been sweetness, chatting wittily about the adventures she had drawn me into over our years together.

I felt contentment settle on me. Life would have been so much duller without her. Sometimes, when I returned to the set of rooms that I shared with her brother Sherlock, I found it flat. Much talk, food for the mind, but flat. He was a man for whom the fair sex had little attraction and Scarlett, I regret to say, was the probable cause. When they had been children together, their mother, Sherlock had told me, had little time for them and expected Scarlett, as the older by two years, to be the stand-in mother. The despotic young girl had taken advantage.

My own experience was of a clever redhead with a waspish wit who could fascinate men. My year or so of endeavours as her faithful admirer were coming to fruition, or so it seemed. Scarlett, when wined and dined well enough to surfeit a princess, could loosen her hair and some of her whale bones too. Bed she said – what bliss.

'John, look at this flower display – isn't it just perfect? Here it says that the trumpet can be a foot long and can be white or purple-tinged or even a glorious orange red. We could grow some ourselves in the university gardens, they would be magnificent.

'They are called angel's trumpets,' she continued. 'They were grown by the Aztecs for their erotic fumes. We could plant some together; I need you with me while we do it together - the exudations of the leaves can be poisonous. I have been allowed a bed for some of my investigations in botany.'

Note: Angel's trumpets have alkaloids – scopolamine. They have been mixed with tobacco to drug wives and slaves so they could be buried alive.

Scarlett & The Secrets

For all their presentation of innocence, girls, women, and with them, Scarlett, can spark trouble. In an expansive moment the lady started telling me about one of her less savoury propensities:

'I started collecting secrets when I was six years old. Secrets were currency, John.' Her face gleamed. 'It was fun to find out things that my brother Sherlock would not want our parents to know.'

'What were they?'

'I could threaten him and have him do things. Sometimes I had him do things that were so bad, I could use them to force him to reveal even worse things.' She grinned like a satyr. 'Boys are stupid, John.'

This exceptional lady was quite outspoken – she would be unconcerned with the jarring effect of such remarks on the men about her. She had festered resentment about men since being expected to confine herself to lady-like attainments. If she were not so devilishly attractive, one could be driven away. As it was, this added piquancy to her personality – something like a meal of peppered wasps.

'You are harsh Scarlett. *He* could only have been four or five years old. As for stupid: boys do grow and catch up with the girls in their university years.'

'Only because they keep girls out of the locus of learning.'

If she had allowed herself to spit, she could have out-shot a camel. Time to change the subject.

'Is that how you came to clandestine work?'

Scarlett ignored my question. - that was an answer in itself. She leaned back with a silent smirk while roaming in her mind. After a few moments, her finger traced a line on the tablecloth. It seemed to leave the impression of an octopus – a cunning creature. My lady was never one to hide her light, not that it always illuminated. In fact, it usually left shadows.

'Secrets can be fashioned, John, like a china figurine. Those skills that I sharpened on Sherlock have served me well. Diplomatic corridors are thick with partial truths.'

I raised my eyebrows.

'They sketch possibilities and bring their subject to accept them. It does not need the whole truth, John; belief is a relief to the troubled mind. I just prepare the minds. I have employed disadvantage to advantage.'

The teacup rattled as I picked it up. This woman had power and she knew it. Being her friend was like being a royal courtier:

so close to power, one could be revered in their magnificence – or lose one's head.

'I had better not ask whom you have manipulated, Scarlett – state secrets, no doubt?'

The wisp of a smile appeared, and she rested her hand on mine. It was smooth and comforting, like the fur on a tiger's paw.

'Well dear lady, for myself I am but a simple man. I have no secrets, nor any influence among the mighty, so I cannot be of interest to your friends in dark circles. As for medical consultations, they are dull and confidential.'

She looked at me from under her eyebrows. She did that when she had something in mind for me to do. 'You could steer my brother, with a remark about his vulnerabilities - to help me,'

'Good heavens, I have ethics and family reputation, more, he is my friend.'

She raised her eyebrows. 'I wonder how your medical practice would get on if certain things became known? Have you never helped a wayward daughter with unwanted motherhood?'

I blanched.

Scarlett had a lever on me.

Note: Terminations were illegal but widespread. Doctors did sometimes act in cases of venereal disease. Some women used Towle's Pills.

Scarlett & The Romans

According to the Times, their lordships had been coughing and retching from a wafting mephitis that had the flavour and force of brown. In the baking heat of a previous summer, the windows of Parliament had, whenever they had been opened, allowed in the fetor that rose from the turbid brown water of the Thames.

The lurid prose in the paper described the doused curtains that had been hung over the windows. They had been quite ineffectual because the water they were wetted with in bucketfuls was the very same liquid that flowed in the London River. Having ignored it for years, of course, that paper could now be wise. They said that from medieval times, even as the city grew, the privies close to the river had dropped straight into it while those near had been piped to it. I, myself, had seen patches of effluent floating across the water, to and fro with the tide. One only had to cross a bridge to know that the odour was rich.

The result, so I read, was that their Lordships had been moved. They had voted to spend large sums on building sewers though the city and sending it all east for purification and to the sea. London was agog with it all: roads would be dug for with trenches and navies would be here in armies.

Scarlett, the archaeologist, wanted to see under the paving. She thought that Roman drains under Londinium were bound to be found. The Romans had laid drains two thousand years ago. She wanted to associate her name with the opening up of Roman engineering under London. A scientific investigation led by *her* and read to scientific bodies would bring her fame.

Here in Marylebone, they were digging a deep trench. Scarlett insisted on going there; she had come to dig in the diggings. I, of course, had to be her assistant. The excuse was my being a doctor and an associate of the well-known detective Sherlock Holmes. She said bodies of the more recent dead might be found. He would be in his element and save her the bother.

The navies had found terracotta pipes, and she was claiming ownership. We took the omnibus to the excavations.

'Look John: drains.'

'Well, we are within the city walls. The drains will go down to the river, just as they have done for years. Not much for the Romans to teach us here.'

'Cesspits, John. I suspect they had cesspits to collect it and make it into manure to be laid on fields.'

'No improvement there – Pepys's neighbour let his cesspit soak into Samuel's cellar.'

'Scoundrel. That man should have paid the night-soil men to scoop it into a tub.'

'Cheaper if he took a few bricks out at the bottom to lose the liquid.'

'That is why we have drains, John.'

'Into the river?'

'These pipes will lead to a cesspit. That is what I say.'

Scarlett was never actually wrong; one had to accept that or take up human flight for a hobby.

'Our engineers are so clever, Scarlett – they have built magnificent bridges, canals and now sewers you could drive a steam train though. The ones they are building along this road have brick arches that rival the cathedrals.'

'The Romans did all that, John'.

Scarlett was right about the Roman cesspit. She found she was crouching in it, Roman effluent and all.

Note: A third-century AD stone building was unearthed, including a subterranean drainage culvert which carried dirty water south from Cornhill to the Thames.

Scarlett & The God Thor

Iron angles buckled. Rivets popped out of beams to fall and clatter on the roof like grape shot. They rolled down the windows in the wash of drenching rain. Scarlett and I were snugged in the warmth of a railway carriage, making our way over the Firth to Scotland. High as we were, up in the air, our train had to forge its way through cascades of spindrift. Foliage flew by, caught in the bouts of howling from the hurricane. The carriage lurched as fists of wind punched it sideways. Way below us rows of waves raced across the Tay. The river was raging at our lofty presumption. We could see wild crests break in the skimming wind, flinging their spume aloft. It was as if a frenzied animal was eating us.

Around, above, ahead, and behind, even below us, the thick darkness was riven with flashes. I was minded of the wrath of Thor. The carriage rocked again. In our fear, we clung together tighter than we ever had, in the embrace of parting.

Scarlett had insisted on taking the train across that long, long bridge. She had the boldness of a warrior, but here we humans were as ants. We were venturing on a spindly lacework of steel; we were intruding where eagles feared to fly.

My brave lady had wanted to hear wind ululating through the bracing, see the sea wrap foamy fingers around those tall, tall stone piers.

'It will be glorious, John. Engineering is the magnificent work of man.'

'You are not a man; you are a lady and an archaeologist, not an engineer.'

'Fiddlesticks! Anything a man can do; *I* can do better. All the Roman engineers were women.'

My brow must have ruckled. 'Was that true?'

'They must have been, the aqueducts are so elegant, the men just did the digging.'

I shrugged but did so while clinging onto a window strap. It hung in front of the door, like the nose of a deflated elephant.

My shrugging jerk released the window. It clunked down and the gale blew in.

'John! Close the window!'

I was struggling with the strap, trying to haul it back up. The carriage rocked again and lifted and twisted and bucked. As I wrestled, the door swung open, with me hanging on to it. Scarlett reached out to grasp my jacket. The whole carriage swayed again, and we both were flung into the roaring abyss.

It was in times like these that one uttered one's most fervent prayer. I was a regular attender, at least on Sundays – some of my patients needed divine intersession. I sought respite from the God who made the wind and the waters, and they told me, man too.

My prayers were answered. After punishing us for challenging the wind, that same power dropped us onto the ballast along the side of the track. It was bruising. Scarlett dropped on top of me.

The train rattled and clatterd. The hammers of Hell were beating on their anvils. then: silence. Only the moaning misery of the wind remained. What we could see of the oil lamps on the back of the disappearing guard's van shook and flickered. As we lay, we suffered the deluge and the bruises, cursing our mess and our foolhardiness. Wet and weary, we watched the rear lamps of that warm dry carriage train dwindle in the increasing distance.

In the next impossible moment, they arced downwards. Flames roared from the engine and bodies leapt out. The sight, though it lasted only seconds, was magnificent and, only when horror caught the thought, totally tragic. No one in the carriages could escape. No one who would plunge into those angry waters could reach for a gulp of air. It was a theatre of death.

We lay, unable to move, unable to speak. Around us the lightning crackled still – dancing from rivet to rivet. Below, the carriages had become black birds of the black air. Windows aglow with that oily, yellow-framed etiolated faces of helpless passengers. For an eternity of seconds, they prayed and pressed themselves flat against the glass.

I helped Scarlett stand, and we stood on the sleepers. For a full five minutes we puzzled at the odd shapes of tangled steelwork: Thor had crushed it in his mighty fist.

We tramped, sleeper to sleeper back to the land.

Note: The Tay Bridge collapse dropped several spans and a train into the roiling river one exceptionally stormy night in 1879.

Scarlett & The Garrotte

One November evening, Scarlett and I walked into London's theatre district – cabs passed but all were occupied. The play had drawn a considerable audience. Crowds are uncomfortable; they push and mutter. In the thick of it troublesome people lurk. Ahead of us, several earnest groups of men and women had seen our elaborate hats and were pushing up to us. They were holding placards – we were not interested. Distraction was a pickpockets' tactic.

One insolent fellow in a grubby bowler was intent on forcing himself and his wretched cause on to us. He took umbrage at my dismissal of his moral rectitude. His rotund and equally ignorant woman bothered Scarlett with some similar grievance. They swore at us. It was intolerable.

I tugged my lady away and led her around a corner into a street populated only by plane tees. It was a side street of well-to-do houses with basements and iron railings. The pavement was empty; we were safer there. We could walk on in peace and find our way around to the theatre at the next turning.

I was looking, trying to read the signpost on the far street, when my head was jerked back. A cord had flicked in front of my eyes, wound round my neck and was now being sawed across my throat. I was pulled back off-balance. My arms jerked out in front and my stick flew out of my hands. I choked. My fingers grabbed at the cord. While my hands were occupied, my wretched assailants pulled my jacket down my arms and rooted in my waistcoat for sovereigns. More maulers prised the notecase out of my jacket. In the blackness of the moment, I could think of nothing, not even one Holmes's Bartitsu tricks he'd taught me.

Scarlett, aware of the sudden capture of me, wheeled round and swung the expensive black boot on her free leg into the skirts of the big biddy behind me. There was an animal howl, and I was let go. A second drive with this same flying foot had the other molly spread-eagled onto the spears of the iron railings. The first one let go of the cord around my neck. The second dropped my notecase to the pavement, and the third, my double Hunter.

The rotund one screeched and pounded fat fingers on Scarlett's back. Now that my own arms were free, I could pull her off. In a matter of moments, the gang had scrambled away, followed by the shrill sound of police whistles. I turned a quizzical eye to my elegant lady in her abundant skirts.

'Savate, John. I went to a French finishing school'.

Note: Savate is a French martial art which combines punching with kickboxing. It was founded in 1838 by Charles Lecour.

Scarlett & The Balloon

Flight was a wonderful invention, and as soon as it was practical, women wanted to get into it.

'Stay there, John'.

Without concern for any response, Scarlett climbed out of the basket. She was upon some errand of her own. As so often with a lady *the man* had to wait. I sat on the leather binding at the opposite corner, making notes of the experience. I had the idea of recommending the contrivance to my regiment as a means of observing the Afghans hiding in their hills.

The envelope above us had been filled with an airy substance through a hose from a lumbering generator on wheels. The whole resembled an elephant taking snuff. We had been about to cast off, indeed several of the ropes were slithering in the grass as the wind took hold of the vast sphere of rubberised silk above us. We moved. I suppose the rigger who had been holding us down, had fallen over when the big basket bumped him. Without Scarlett's weight and with this gust, we – or rather *I* was buoyant. A sharp thrill shivered my legs. This was like having one's foot tangled in the stirrup of a bolting horse. Earthly existence was over, death invited. A broken body was the future.

I shouted; I had to do *something*. Scarlett usually took a few minutes to return from her sudden expeditions, but this time, with her skirts clasped in her hands, she returned at the run.

The last rope was dangling, and the basket was skidding across the grass in the manner of a swan running, wings spread, ready to soar into the clouds. I was to rise to Heaven unshriven.

'I told you to wait for me!' Scarlett stepped on the recumbent rigger, the better to jump, and took hold of the rope. In the manner of a competent horsewoman, she spoke to the balloon in a firm but calming voice. The great aero bag drooped, obedient to her word, and a weakening wind. Scarlett swung her other leg into the basket and returned to my company.

'By Jove, Scarlett, you are a sporting lass.'

'You can drop a sandbag now, John, to get over those trees.'

We ascended and the people shrank to Lilliputians. It was all instructive for my notes. My lady friend was scowling.

'Where did you think you were going, John? You cannot just leave a lady like that; it is not gentlemanly.'

'But I, you, I . . . '

'Just do not do it again, John.'

Note: Victorian men and women were intrigued with the possibilities of flight by hydrogen balloons. The British Association even developed a Balloon Committee.

Scarlett & The Arcade

The horse snickered. Ahead of me Scarlett slipped into a passageway just a few steps from an arcade in Piccadilly. She had not noticed my cab or if she had, she was discrete. I had been called to make a morning visit to the overdecorated rooms that lay behind the arcade. The medical fees these rooms could pay me, compensated for the pro-bono visits I made to the workhouses.

Close, personal, private examinations were made in these rooms. Sometimes, also a little dose of mercury. The reputation of those within amongst the gentry that they dealt with depended on my services. Medical discretion meant that I made little mention of such visits, even to Holmes, and never to his sister Scarlett. I would be misunderstood.

A purchase of jewellery was the usual reason given by a gentleman for a visit to these ornate shops. Those still undecided about how many carats would be enough, could take tea or, for a larger purchase, perhaps a comforting glass in a viewing room at the back. In other rooms, yet further back, the fall of a necklace or the scintillation of a sapphire brooch could be seen gracing a delicate neck. Making a choice could be tiring and often took until the clock chimed again.

For the convenience of customers or friends, as they became, so satisfactory were their purchases, the establishment, along with several others in the arcade, was open quite late into the evening. Men of business late from their offices, or gentlemen early for the theatre or cards at their club, were accommodated. The reputation was of the highest and murmured of only between men of significance.

It was pleasure for me, an impoverished professional, to pretend to purchase in *this* particular shop, so elegant were the beauties who were fêted there. The consulting rooms were above, so having selected a few brooches, the jewel expert holding them in her white gloved fingers on a velvet cushion would lead me to the stairs. After my professional work, a small brooch might be the reward I could show in my hand, as if it were a purchase.

Leaving one of the rooms was, I was sure because of his curling moustache, a fellow from the Hungarian embassy. No doubt he was buying for his wife. Less happy was I about the elegant back, and the gown that flowed down it, that so resembled the person at the pinnacle of my affections. A bolt of jealousy shot through me.

Jitters shook my focus and I hoped I would not be asked to make an examination. It was not unknown for ladies to become lost in the warren of rooms while seeking personal facilities. The establishment provided also for ladies who wished to provide something special for their friends.

The beauty turned and put a long finger across her lips. A cloud of perfume enveloped me when she whispered in my ear.

'John, the Hungarian Second Secretary is an informant to me on Russian secret policy. I use the girls like spiders to trap them in their peccadillos.'

Note: Honeytraps were used by women from the age of Catherine de Medici to the age of Queen Victoria. The former had a band of female intelligencers who were also operators. Queen Vitoria had information sources at high level throughout Europe through her family. These she fed to the prime minister of the day and influenced policy.

Scarlett & The Bombers

The stair creaked at each step. A tiny but annoying echo off the grimy walls reflected each small noise right up the wooden stairs to a closed door above. While standing with the police beside the back door, I had to watch Scarlett's progress. My job was to distinguish good from bad amongst the hellcats who would emerge, in a great rush. My service revolver was held hidden.

The forces of order were there to bundle bombers into the Black Maria outside. They had been spotted arriving and the police had been informed. How many – ten, fifteen? Some more might have been here for some time, hiding.

Footfalls could be distinctive. Would they have recognised the cadence of her steps? Would they have burst out and attacked that brave woman?

A cold shiver shook me – these soldiers of the Devil, spilling down the stairs after grappling with her, might then set upon me. I am a respectable gentleman of, I supposed I could call it, early middle age. While I had been a soldier years ago, I was not an infantry man. Horrors, would I be able to fight off ten of those insane amazons? My gammy leg felt weak at the thought of it.

That shudder freed another thought in me as I imagined being pinned on the floor by a vigorous woman in the bloom of her passion. Matron had been in her bloom, as I recall. She enjoyed chastising boys. The sting stayed with me still.

The reverie broke. It was a grey late afternoon in an empty office building in South London. Elsewhere, honest men would be at their labours and honest women – at their charities. Here we were stalking vicious lawbreakers whispering their plots, snarling and sharpening their claws like pumas.

Bombers are reputed to creep upon their victims in the dark. Scarlett was on a mission for one of the closed corridors of government. By insinuating herself into places where she could listen, she could report on anarchist plans for explosions. Here she must have heard enough for be a witness for the prosecution.

A shrill police whistle rent the air. In the dim light from a sooty glass skylight, I saw Scarlett, her hand to her mouth. She was blowing the alarm and covering her face from recognition before slipping away, flattening herself against the wall beyond the door.

The bombers burst out, shouting abuse against the authorities. Poor brave Scarlett. I had my heart in my mouth. I started up the stairs to rescue her. Foolish, for it made *me* the visible enemy. They missed her and saw me! They poured down the stairs. The first fists blooded my ear and knocked my hat off. I cringed, I could not retaliate, despite Holmes's lessons in Bartitisu. I had no umbrella to wield or rolled newspaper with which to belabour them. As I collapsed under the hoard, arms tangled in knots, my finger squeezed my trusty revolver.

To my tousled relief, the bang was quite enough in that narrow stair shaft, the powder flash sounded and looked like a howitzer. The women screamed, holding their ears. My own had already been blocked with a female fist at that instant, as well as the pile of fragrant flesh pressing against my face. They smothered all sensation – a brief but beautiful moment.

The policemen tumbled in. The shocked tigresses were clapped in cuffs and hauled away in the Black Maria outside.

Scarlett had kept herself out of their vision. She would testify behind a screen in the magistrate's court.

Note: In 1881, " the slogan "propaganda of the deed" was adopted by the anarchist London Congress. It included bombings and tyrannicides.

Scarlett & The Fund

The day was dreary. Scarlett and I were being jolted across the East End. On each side of the four-wheeler, lanes between rows of mean houses were crammed with sad sights: poor people, emaciated, with clusters of bony children.

'Scarlett, people should eat more fruit.'

'An apple a day keeps the doctor *away*. Is that what you want, Doctor Watson?'

'I was thinking of the poor. They only get bread and tea, then they get rickets.'

'There is no fruit grown in London.'

'Coster mongers bring apples on barrows for those who can spare a farthing.'

'There is not much in an apple, John.'

'My journal says they have vitamins. If the poor would eat fruit, they would be less ill and so less poor.'

'What about pineapples? I read that they are beneficial for all sorts of conditions.'

'Exotic, Scarlett. People pay a fortune just to hire one to show off at a dinner party.'

'Better to bring in pineapples then, John. According to the paper, there is a fellow growing them in South America. He needs investors. There you are: good works and profits, too.'

'This sounds like the Darien Scheme – it failed.'

'That was mismanaged.' She folded back the newspaper and read the investment page. 'Here is a scheme in Poyais. You could invest and make a fortune in a year or two. Look, it says that it is being managed by a Scottish businessman. He says he is the Cazique – the ruler of a tract of prime land in Central America where it is hot with lots of rainfall. He says that it is rich farming land. All we have to do is clear the jungle, fence out the animals and plant the pineapples.'

'I am not a farmer.'

'John, you do not have to be. They do it. It says here all they do is take some fruits to start, cut off the body of the thing, then poke the stem into the ground. After that they multiply – easy-peasy.'

'Well, it does sound easy.'

'It says here the land is a paradise: warm and friendly with fruit growing in abundance. Instead of living in wet and smoky London, you could start a practice out there. You could spend your days in comfort and happiness. Who would *not* want to live in peace and idleness in the South Seas?'

'Do they have dancing girls with swooping loops of flowers and big smiles.'

'I can see that you are warming to this, John. Just think, you could cash that army pension and live well there for the rest of your life.'

'Have you explained your investment idea to your brother?'

'I said *I* could invest all his money for him, for a fee of course, but he was *very* rude to me.'

Note: Overseas planation investments were profitable, but the Darian scheme was a trick. In times of slow communication, investors had no way of knowing what was happening far away on the ground. Scots invested handsomely in Darian – many nations of that era wanted colonies, an empire perhaps, lands overseas or at least the profits of plantations, as well as trade from far-flung lands. The failure of this scheme bankrupted Scotland and led to the Union.

Scarlett & Prince Albert

The newspaper had a black headline.

'John, poor Prince Albert has died: typhoid. Our dear Queen will be distraught. Is there no cure?'

'Scarlett, typhoid arises from accumulation of sewage. The health of London demands that we install piped drainage to all the houses. We still have gong farmers at night shovelling waste from cellars into carts. The stench around those houses is redolent of a farmyard – no wonder the ladies carry posies. The loaded carts spill onto the road and it all mixes what the horses leave. The sweepers, little fellows, work hard if you give them a coin, but they cannot clean it all out of the cobbles – as the fringes of my patients' skirts will attest. When they enter my rooms . . ,'

'Enough, John! It would cost a fortune to dig drains into all the streets, not to mention the disruption of the traffic.'

'It would also cause a disruption to the houses, Scarlett, but it must be done. We have epidemics. You have contacts in the corridors of government. Can you not speak to them?'

'John, no urging moves government money. It always needs a political driver – something has to happen.'

'There are privies *in* the Parliament buildings, I suppose. Their lordships would not go outside.'

'Do the gong farmers carry full baskets along the corridors at night? Their lordships sit late.'

'Scarlett, you were reading about Ephesus. Did they have gong farmers?'

'No, clay drains, flushed by the water supply – nearly three thousand years ago.'

'Well, the Palace of Westminster is beside the Thames, so I imagine their privies drop into drains. When it storms, the flow from rain would wash it all into the river. No baskets slopping in the corridors.'

'But an awful odour in this summer drought.'

Scarlett stiffened statue still – that noesis thing of hers. She had deep insights. I have learned better than to break those spells. Her temper if interrupted, was like flying shards of glass.

'John, I have an idea. Something to create a political driver, something to blast their lazy lordships into action.'

'You are going to shriek in the chamber?'

'They would think me a mad woman.'

'Then how will you move the minister?'

'My bestial brother is, or was, a chemist. That is before he took to strutting about. He once told me that methane is powerfully explosive. When it seeps into a coal mine, their oil lamps can set it off. It blasts right back from the coal face and sends the bodies back like bullets.'

'Bullets are not the way to address Parliament, Scarlett. That happens in Russia or France; this is England.'

'Well John, if you could sneak into the building and bail out the water traps under the privies, then the sewer gasses will slowly fill those small, tiled rooms. We need to do it before the rain washes the piles away. That evening, when the minister enters with his lighted candle, the china bowl will speak volumes to him.'

Note: In 1861, Prince Albert died of typhoid in Windsor castle. The disease was widespread and killed a third of those infected. Lack of foul drains and a treatment system was the cause. The Great Stink from the Thames, which was overloaded with sewage from the discharge of drains from the rapidly expanding population, brought the problem right into the Houses of Parliament. Their lordships funded the start of trunk sewer construction.

150

Scarlett & The Babies

Scarlett had an impatient view of children. It seemed to have arisen from her pubescent annoyance with her younger brother Sherlock. She was more mature, and moody too – or so *he* told me.

At that age, she was also bigger and could bully him. Sherlock had been admonished not to hit girls, whereas *she* felt free to pinch him painfully – out of parental sight, of course – if he failed to obey her. She threatened to do worse if he were to reveal her misdeeds. Of course, their mother was predisposed to believe girls to be blameless angels. That experience seemed to have taught her a lot about how females could manipulate males – and eat the fruit of it.

All this came to mind as she talked of the Warlock family; the whisper was in every parlour. Scarlett wore a mischievous expression – she did that when she wanted to prise private information out of me. She took my arm.

'We women know that a man is easily diverted by a pretty face like those voluptuous maids who have taken village boys, then pushed them aside.' I was warming to her theme:

'And wayward young daughters, Scarlett, who grow up in a house with tall footmen.' I suspected a scandal. My ears pricked. I had to add words of caution:

'It all goes wrong. Scarlett, unmarried servants who become pregnant are dismissed. No other house will employ them, their reputation would taint the family – what else might happen if such a loose girl were to be loose in the house? If they are to be employed somewhere, they have to give away their child to a foundling hospital.' It did not divert her.

'John, Lady Warlock's daughter has gone to the country. The girl is known to you, I think?'

'I saw her a month ago, looking a little fuller in the figure than she was. She might be away for some months.'

'No more riding to hounds for a while. Eh?'

'I advised her to find new friends. She could get away from the servants, grooms can become overfamiliar. There are village women who can help a rash girl, can *you*?'

'There is little *I* can offer in the surgery: abortion is illegal. I usually advise them to go to the country – somewhere discreet, but I suspect some such girls, in the dark of the morning take their poor little charge to the foundling hospital. They do not have to reveal who they are – they knock on a door low in the wall and speak through a grille. The door opens and a narrow table appears upon which they place the bundle. The door closes and they have soothed their conscience. It is a place where the infant could be fed and comforted, but too many tiny necks are vulnerable to heavy hands.'

Note: The population, particularly of London, doubled in the century - there was no contraception or abstinence. Servants were not permitted followers or children, so their accidental babies were sometimes abandoned, mostly to orphanages or to women who took a fee for housing them. Some did not survive.

Scarlett & The Diary

I was in Scarlett's study at Newnham college. Why was I there? She had written me a very terse note: 'Come at once.' It was a style typical of her brother, but where he was brief, she was commanding.

I arrived in the late evening because I had taken the first available train. I was not allowed to see her in her rooms. The college servant – a short, doughty woman, who could have felled an ox with a glance – blocked the whole of the corridor with her scowl.

'She's having a turn – shut herself away.'

'I'm a doctor.'

'Then go to her study, she will come to you.'

So, there I was, sitting at *her* desk, in *her* chair, worried about her, wanting to help, having been asked to attend and yet having to diagnose her condition in her absence. What could I do? As chance would have it, in front of me was her diary. Diaries were private, but a quick look might give me a clue. It seemed to be my duty.

'Dear diary,' were the words last written, "My secret is so burdensome.' The writing was spidery: blots and inkless scratches The *woman* in Scarlett feared something.

Having evoked Sherlock, his hurt memories of Scarlett that he had revealed to me pointed to her burden of guilt. It could hang like a thunder cloud, constantly threatening to deluge and drown her. On the widow to her study, the rain outside poured as if from that very cloud. This perhaps was the root of her negativity with men – heavy guilt. Now I could do something.

As her admirer, and a doctor, I would try to ease her aversion and bring her home to harbour.

The next line was even more troubling: 'Will they forgive me?'

Poor Scarlett, dear sweet lady.

'I have sinned.' Well, that was certainly true. Maybe the realisation of her bad behaviour would open the way for me to be her confessor.

Forgiveness without penance had no traction on the mind, no restoration to the suffering – the church urges it.

Door hinges behind me creaked like a scream.

'John! What are you doing with my diary!'

'Oh! Er, I'm sorry!'

'Mind your own business!'

'Sorry, I was only trying to help. You asked me to come urgently. You seem to be troubled.'

'I need you, not that pompous brother of mine. I need a soldier.'

'What?!' I did not want to shoot anybody.

'It is to do with some work I did for government.'

Hmm, clandestine activities, *again.*

'I need a military man to stand for me. I set some people against each other with a secret their enemies wanted. One of them is looking for me in Cambridge. I want you lecture in my place for a few days. Best to wear a bone corset and several thick waistcoats in case of a swordstick.'

Note: The swordstick was a popular fashion accessory for the wealthy during the 18th and 19th centuries, even for some women.

Scarlett & The Woods

This November day was bright; soft, fragrant air riffled our hair. The scent of mould was rising from the mulch of autumn leaves. It filled me deeply. I was walking close to Scarlett while she was leading led the way between the many trees. Leaves were falling; at each step my shoes lifted sprays of brown and gold. We were as happy as children, even though the branches above us were as the dark fingers of a medieval nursery rhyme, pressing down on us.

My lady delighted in the flitting contrasts: boles of trees once lighted by shafts of sun were, in the next moment, merged into the dull crowd of its fellows. In the next moment, they would reappear as if alive. Those shadowing branches moved aside by gusts of wind. To her, they were moving as ghosts did: humans seen in memory. A good claret, taken with the beef pie, had fuelled our imaginations.

With ever an eye to history, the lady archaeologist spoke of the past.

'Woods were dangerous places, John. They cover so much of England and harbour evil. The folk memories are with us still. Remember the Babes in the Wood? Did you recite that in the nursery? It was a warning to the unknowing.'

And a lure for the naughty.

'They remain dangerous, Scarlett. Your brother had a case —'

A stiff gloved hand stopped me.

'Huh! He is lost in the present; he knows nothing of how we all got here. People grow out of the land, John: tradition, farming, villages lost under tangles of brambles.' She turned to me with mischief in her eye. 'There are leafy dells here, John, where villagers went to dance. Women led their menfolk into them, one hand holding the man, the other – a jar of fresh ale.'

The wind was as a choir, singing softly like a mistress impatient to glory her senses. My blood pulsed. The lady was a temptress. I was eager to respond, but not too seriously. If I had mistaken her, harsh words would tear at my ears, tearing flesh – thorns on brambles.

'Witchcraft is over with, Scarlett, surely.' My tone was more questioning than conclusive – months earlier, over a bacchanalian dinner party she had revealed to me that a coven at her school had cultivated a cult of coquetry. They had practised it on the old gardener. He died of blood pressure, the doctor said. The girls knew why.

This lady had depth and feminine skills.

'Jeremiah, verse nineteen: "I will cause them to eat at the flesh of the sons and the flesh of the daughters."'

What did she mean eat? Was she alluding to, inviting me, tempting me to explore pagan excesses?

'There is danger here, John.'

Yes, yes, my queen. I could feel it – my limbs tingled. Danger heightens the senses. I was being drawn, pulled, seduced. My propriety crumbled. I was entranced, willing, eager to be her sacrifice. I followed her into a ring of trees on a slight rise, towards a fold in the ground.

'Here we can do something you will enjoy.' She sank to the earth and brushed at the soft leaves, her feline form gracing the ground. 'Doctor, sit beside me. Look, just here. I have brought you to a place where your fingers can feel a sacrificial skull.'

Note: Samhain is a Greater Sabbat – the spirits of the dead are to attend.

Scarlett & Childhood

On this dank day, Scarlett had a fever. She had called for me, more, I suspect, for my medical assistance than my companionship, but well, half a loaf.

The patient was in her lodgings at Cambridge – a wood panelled room, heavy with the sharp scent of lavender. It was reached by stone corridors and creaking oak stairs.

The college servant scowled when I arrived at the gate and bustled me into Scarlett's room only when that echoey corridor was quite empty. A ladies' college only admitted men within their walls in the direst circumstance.

As we walked, the woman seethed like a wet log on a fire, hissing something about women too being allowed to study medicine. I suggested they also take up plumbing. Her snort silenced my sentence, so I told the insolent woman that she could help at the bedside, with towels to absorb the sweats, and in particular those tasks associated with the need of drains.

Instead, a char from the town was summoned. Remarkably ugly, she filled the other side of the room. At my instance, her chair was pushed back into the shadow.

I applied my medical experience to cool Scarlett's fever. It was of excellent avail: my lady spoke. Her delirium began to pour out of her. Her voice, now begun, was weak and faltering – sweetly feminine, I thought. It warmed my heart, if only she would adopt it for ever afterwards – a sort of epiphany. I bent over her pale, pretty face the better to hear. Delirium is revealing. Should I have listened? I was a doctor; it was my duty. She murmured something about baby Sherlock. Saying his name made her splutter; so many sibilants, I supposed. Moisture beaded on my poor, suffering enchantress's brow. What was she confessing to me? I felt like a priest being begged for absolution – forgiveness for her heart.

'The new baby stole my place.'

'What's that, Scarlett?'

She arched up in the bed, straining the words through clamped teeth.

'That wretched boy. *I* was the apple. *I* was the favourite. Then *he* arrived. All their attention turned to him. *I* was forgotten. They kept saying: "A Boy, A Boy,". I *hate* small boys.' She coughed.

'Scarlett do not distress yourself. Not all boys are…' I did not want her to view me in this dark light.

'Ha! They gave him everything. I was much cleverer. Now, he just potters, with *crime* of all things. I am a reputable academic! As children I could beat him at everything AND I told

164

him that., he is not happy about that. Perhaps you and your brother could be reconciled ...'

A demonic grin crossed her face.

'He is too guilty to be a friend, so I torment him.'

'What?'

'Give me a drink, John. Gin. the sorority swears by it.'

The bottle was on her bedside table. I handed it to her. She drank and continued.

'He told mother lies about me, the weed. He did not hit me, but *mother* did – she used her hairbrush while she bent me over her knee. It was painful. I had red skin afterwards. His piffling scars would mend. My dignity was wounded for ever. I was only having fun with him. We were playing doctors. I wanted to play the surgeon – it was only a carrot knife.'

Was it why Holmes's had no use for women?

Note: Gynophobia is a fear of women, more precisely the fear men experience of being humiliated by women, particularly by emasculation.

Scarlett & The Graves

We arrived at a station halt, miles into the countryside, late in the afternoon of a winter's day. Scarlett had persuaded me to accompany her on grim errand. She had determined to investigate a premonition she had had during one of her séances.

We alighted onto the platform with our small suitcases, gathering up our hats, sticks and scarves. The night air was crisp, it drained what heat we had absorbed from the fug in the train. Wasting no time, as there were no new passengers, the guard blew his whistle and waved his green flag. For a moment there was bustle. The engine blasted a cloud of steam across the planks of the platform and turned its great wheels.

The carriages passed us one by one, clunking over the track joints as it sped up. The train left us with no farewell but the reddish light of a meagre tail lamp that shook and dwindled and soon disappeared.

In the blackness of night, we were alone. No station staff, no signal box at the end of the platform, not even a gas lamp to light the narrow plankway that did duty as a platform at such unfrequented stations. I struck a match. It flared, fizzled and died, doing little to frighten away the engulfing darkness.

Glistening wet, wooden steps took us down to the stony lane and we stood there for fully a minute to decide whether we preferred the hopelessness of one way rather than the helplessness of the other. Cold seized us as we considered, but we began to discern the edges of the hedges against the only somewhat lesser dark of the wintery sky.

Scarlett announced her decision in tones as though she had always known and strode out. I, of course, had no voice at all. This was her mission and she had, as usual, explained nothing to me, just having told me in her regal manner to come. Fool man, why do I do it? She used me. Yet, I would follow her to the abyss.

She declared that we had to turn left and march to the village whose lights we could see, or rather *she* said *she* could see between the distant trees. For myself, I would have been happier waiting for the next train, whenever that might be.

The lane was rutted and trapped with potholes. It took us what turned out to be a mile before the trees parted to reveal a village. Oil lamps stood in windows offering a soft light that beguiled us to rest and warm by firesides within. Scarlett would have none of it. She wanted to visit the churchyard by night. Night was realm of the occult. She believed she had connections with such things – at least, she let others believe it so. We saw the steeple and struck out for the churchyard. What passed there turned my hair white.

We pushed at an iron gate in brick wall that leaned unhappily outwards as if it could hardly contain what was within. The gate resisted us but gave at last with small shriek as the old metal broke its bonds of rust. Where were we to look first?

Graveyards contained layers of bodies. In times past, the Reaper had laid them in the earth with a wooden cross or maybe nothing at all to mark the being and passing of each soul to the Heaven they so sought above. Some premonition had Scarlett point to the far corner, farthest away from the holiness of the church and up against the weary old wall.

Here were gravestones, a row of them, all the same shape and size and colour. Scarlett had reasoned that they must have been erected at the same date and for some same purpose. Perhaps we had found the place to which her doleful voices had led her. She hung her head and muttered words in ecclesiastical Latin.

These grey flat memorial stones of no great height were leaning backwards. Their crumbling faces were dully to be glimpsed in the moonlight when the smothering cloud parted above us. A bitter wind repeatedly punched the cedar tree that guarded the corner. Sweeping low branches crossed graves long forgotten. Bare of leaves, twigs scratched away at the stone words like the arthritic fingers of the Reaper.

Bodies had been buried there, so Scarlett told me. Young bodies, children's bodies, twisted, emaciated bodies. It put in my mind the sight of a faithful dog pawing, clawing at a door, longing for it to open.

Gravel, now infested with weeds, had been spread over the graves. The surface had lifted and rounded from frosts as they expanded the soil beneath. Bodies did not push up from their coffins, even if it looked that way. During the day, jackdaws pecked at the gravel, cawing and pulling at worms. By night, one could indeed imagine stirrings below. The calls of the jackdaws could remind one of children whimpering.

Children had been buried here on just such a night long ago, Scarlett told me. Her research in the ecclesiastical archives had seen it written that in those days the village was remote. The church had been built by a benefactor from another manor. He wanted the Divine to reward him with everlasting life. The humble folk who worked for him would go there to worship the deity, and him.

More was to happen that night. For me, the dark mysteries were uncomfortable and little soothed when Scarlett wove a history of the village for me. It took her most of the journey when we caught the train back. Life for some was little above the animals.

Circumstances did not improve for the villagers after their benefactor had gone to his Maker, so long ago. In those days, life was thin and remote. No one visited the village, not even the peddlers – they who had found few buyers for the wares they had to carry on their backs. The Great Road lay a long away. To reach it took much of a day along a rutted lane that was ankle-breaking in drought and glutinous after rain.

In those bleak years, the village had turned in on itself. The harshness of nature compounded their earthen beliefs. There was now no living for even a Curate. Only when they had something to spare from their labours, and even then, only when the lane was passable, did they send carts of vegetables to the market.

Sometimes the carter did not return. No money or tools or woollen clothing were brought back. The people were poor and simple. Life was simple. They kept to themselves. The hours of night-time were their periods of pleasure. When work was finished in the fields, sweaty bodies went to bed to take their delights there.

Many of the children looked the same, as did those who had begotten and forgotten them when turning over their short generations. Amongst any straggling crowd of youngsters, young mothers could not be certain which of the children were their own – they all lived so closely together. In a kindly way, they all tended to all of the little ones while the men worked in the fields.

Amongst these were some who stood rather shorter than the others, lovable and needing love. It was a small village and far from the road. Love was all they had.

Scarlett, the historian, had lost herself in recounting their miseries. Our train rattled over points. In the jerking clatter, she returned from her disconsolate mood to come to the point of this grim outing.

Few had stood by the graveside on an evening years ago when those four were buried. The funeral service had been conducted in the dark. Owls had called and swooped in the woods. The mourners had found their way by flickering candles, protected from the icy wind in iron lanterns.

By then the village had dwindled because the farms dwindled and that because fewer and fewer found reward in the land. They had turned to taking their pleasures in gratification of the flesh. The resulting children grew into feckless adults, those who were whole in their being. The sick and odd proliferated and finally for want of energy and understanding, sacrificial ritual was the only hope.

Those four graves held children's bodies. They had been *sacrificed* to placate, to implore, to supplicate, some overarching beings.

Scarlett & The Homeless

It was a rather late when Scarlett sent short note for me to join her. It was to be a tea shop not far from her club. It was indicative, I thought, of what was to be a delicate conversation. An ordinary meeting would have had me summoned me to the intimidating grandeur of her London club.

A cab took me to an elegant tea shop fluttering with ladies. I met a flock of feathered hats. Upon enquiry, I was shown to an alcove right at the back. Scarlett was there, sunken into an engulfing world of brown leather armchairs, surrounded by aspidistras and tucked close to green flock wallpaper. In my mind was the kind of swampy Afghan forestation that could hide a sniper.

'John! I suppose that dilatory brother of mine detained you.'

A reply was not necessary; her expostulation was not unusual. Frequent fault-finding in her younger brother was her habit.

As I looked, her face, though shaded by an ostrich hat, showed puffiness. My diagnostic eye looked for a reason. In her youth, she had been a hard and healthy hockey player and was as fit as a filly.

'My dear lady, whatever has happened? What can I do for you? I infer there is some urgency. How?'

'John do stop wittering. I need quiet assistance and I cannot ask my impecunious brother.'

I confess I smiled; she was to be in my debt. There is no friend like a friend in need. Recollecting myself, I winced and commiserated at her misfortune. She raised an eyebrow over a narrow, black, suspecting eye.

'Listen, don't mumble. I have to leave my lodgings.'

'Your rooms Cambridge? They are commodious and comfortable, what I have seen of them.'

'Yes, and I have been there for years John. I *live* there. It is my nest, my retreat, my place of comfort. Leaving my accustomed home would be such a wrench. Where would I go? Where would I put my books, my certificates, my trophies?' She faltered and her hand rose to cover her moistening eyes. She could not allow even a slight sign of weakness. In my heart, I always knew there was a soul under her carapace or at least I had imagined it so, her being a woman.

My attention was taken for a few moments by our waitress – rather pretty, I thought, in her billowing blouse. Some women resemble ships in full sail.

'John!'

'Scarlett, I have to order some tea, I cannot sit here without asking for what is on offer.'

'Tea is *all* that is on offer. I thought you came here to help me.'

'Yes, of course.' Had I? Yes, I supposed so.

'*Alley cats*! I have suffered academic jealousy: Backstabbing. A manufactured misunderstanding. Some vicious cat has clawed down my reputation. Rumours have been put about. I had been reciting Sappho – such a feline poet, so they say. I have been seen trousered in amorous company; they describe me as dancing à deux in my room. They had that pretty student, the one who jumped up and kissed me in the lecture you gave, to be a witness of my character and proclivities.'

I remembered that that pixie made meal of kissing her – she was supposed to have kissed me when Scarlett came in. That was when I was manoeuvring the wretch to ignite jealousy in Scarlett. The girl had other interests.

'Perish the thought.' She drilled another gimlet look at me. '*You,* John, need to help me expunge these rumours.'

'Well, I could represent you with the chancellor. My standing as military surgeon with the Middlesex regiment should let me talk straight to him.'

'Thank you, dear.'

Dear, she said, what a petal.

'But I don't think they would listen to you, even as old soldier. It is your maleness I need. We would have to be caught *in flagrante delicto* in the Common Room to disprove the rumours.'

'Should I wear my pyjamas?' This was becoming more interesting by the minute.

'No, I shall have to call the staff to witness us, and then I need them to throw you into the street.'

Scarlett & Her Father

My being a doctor made me of use to Scarlett.

'John, I would like you to see my father.'

This seemed quite a step forward in my relationship with this fascinating lady. To meet her father was tantamount to her acceptance of my suit. A tingle of nervousness ran through me; it dried my throat. I could hardly find words.

'Oh Scarlett, I am not sure that I would know what to say to the venerable gentleman.' She had not been explicit about the success of my approach. I did not want to put my foot in it and squander the days, dinners and delights of my careful courtship.

'Fiddlesticks man, you are a doctor.'

This allusion to my medical profession was less warming. Perhaps she just wanted me to examine the old buffer.

'You just need to take him by the hand and see how long he will last.'

Hmm, it was clear she was calculating how long it would be before she came into his money. Scarlett was ever the pragmatist.

'Length of life is not an easy prediction, Scarlett. Is the gentleman unwell?'

'He has been the same for years; whenever I go home, which is not very often, he looks the same to me despite his increasing age.'

'You must be a devoted daughter.' A little praise, mixed with hope about her treatment of male relatives was in order, I thought. 'Is your mother still with us?' It was a tentative enquiry; she had feuded with her mother since childhood. Being so painfully punished for that game of surgeons with her younger brother had rankled with her ever since.

'My mother went to a madhouse.'

That news was too horrible to think about – people had been manoeuvred into the madhouse. Doctor Semmelweis had been, just for insisting on hygiene in labour wards. Had she put her mother away? What would happen to her father? Daughters are supposed to love their fathers, but I was not entirely sure about Scarlett, given her enduring family feud with Sherlock.

'I had indeed better see the old gentleman, we don't want him to become a stiff.' I added a chuckle to muddle and moderate my words, lest it was too close to what she *did* want. A shiver passed through my shoulders as the thought of what contrivance she might have had in mind for me to administer.

'He is at the end of the corridor. His skin is rather leathery. What I want to know about, is his insides – I had him embalmed.'

Scarlett & The Public Dinner

Engineers take us to impossible places.

'John, would you like to join me at a public dinner?'

This was splendid news. It seemed that Scarlett the archaeologist was going to receive acclamation for her work in excavations. She had burrowed her way into archaeology and risen to speak widely to learned societies. I was not at all jealous – the brilliant lady deserved her admiration. I had assisted her in her pursuits and was to receive some prominence by accompanying her at the dinner.

Of course, a reasonable observer might reasonably observe that I deserved similar honour from assisting her brother Sherlock in his detective work – supper, at least. He himself would, I am sure he would have said (indeed, he sometimes has said) that I am the whetstone for his mind. People in certain circles spoke highly of his reputation, but none of me.

No, I was just the biographer, the Boswell. Well, we all had our roles, I supposed.

Now, now, accompanying the sparkling Scarlett was my chance to rub shoulders with men of influence. I would become celebrated – a doctor with a practice in fashionable Baker Street.

'John, are you daydreaming?'

'Well, I was just enjoying the prospect of conversing with all those important people. What is it about, Scarlett? Will you be speaking about a dig?'

'It *is* about a dig, John. We in Britain have achieved so many great advances in so many fields: commerce sport, science, medicine. Wonderful work is being advanced in engineering – so many innovations. I will be speaking about my learned papers.'

'What do you hope to achieve – memberships?'

'Funding is what I want out of these banqueting people. I need a sponsor – women are ignored by the stuffy institutions. If I can charm a duke or the mayor of London or a raffish businessman – someone to lend his name *and* his money, to cover my expedition, and possibly himself, in glory.'

'Expedition!? Are you going to Egypt?' My heart froze. How would I live without the companionship of the mesmeric Scarlett? 'May I accompany you? You will need a doctor.'

'Yes, I have just invited you, silly man.'

'I mean on your expedition.'

'John, expeditions need bravery and endurance. Let us see how you survive the banquet.'

'Survive the banquet? Why, what dangers lurk?'

'Brunel has been down in a diving bell dropping clay bags to seal up the hole.'

'What hole?'

'It's fine, John. Do not worry, it's all done now. It does not interfere with the ships; they just sail on, over the top. He is a very ingenious engineer. He has repaired it. Now, to restart the project, he just *has* to show everyone that there will not be another inrush of water. We will be seated at a great table with the investors We, John, will be among the great and the daring.'

'Well, it will not be stuffy then.'

'The dining table is in the tunnel under the Thames, just twelve feet below the riverbed.'

Note: I K Brunel continued his father's pioneer tunnelling under the Thames. It now takes the underground railway from

Scarlett   *&*   The Cigar

Scarlett opened her lips in a round shape that said a silent 'Ooh'. She lifted her chin. Eager girls did that to beckon a kiss. Standing there, looking at her pouting, I was captured, bound as if by chains of silver. She owned every part of me, engulfed my very soul. The lashes of her greenish eyes brushed over me – I felt the wing feathers of an angel. I was soaring. I leaned towards her. Her chin rose yet higher with those soft red kissing-lips. A moment of ecstasy was to consume me, take me into a forbidden world, lock me into servitude of sensation. As I put my lips together for the kiss, she smiled in her own aura of joy, and . . . puffed out a wavering ring of *smoke*. The halo rose in the warm air, fading, diffusing, disappearing, leaving *nothing* but its tickling fragrance. Gravity called; as cold as a hand, pulling me down from those dreams of Paradise.

Indifference. She was in her own world. Her languid wrist, tracing curves in the air; rich wraiths which, of themselves, spoke of exotic pleasures. Tobacco had relaxed her mind, it cleanses, cares and opens a pale page on which was being painted images in the colours of Heaven. The scent of Havana cigars. I breathed it in as well as she - leaves rolled on the dark thighs of Cuban women - sunlight, warmth, softness, sweetness, heady oblivion.

My straying thoughts of Cuban women had pulled my focus away from *her*. She saw it. Women are jealous. Endless, infinite admiration is their due. Her padded shoulders arched like a rampant eagle. On each side of her nose, gimlet eyes flashed. I had become *prey*. Tobacco had taken Scarlett high into a place she should not be, into ideas too sharp.

I braved that flash and the tensing of her claws. I had to save her, my lovely sybarite, from self-destruction. I was a man. A man had duties, responsibilities.

'Few women smoke, Scarlett, and fewer smoke cigars.'

The lady arched her eyebrows into the dark gothic and her lips pinched her retort.

'I am amongst those Few. I have my own ideas.'

My help, my advice, my fond concern had been rebutted. I gasped. She would be rejected by Society. I tried to explain, 'Smoking is not fashionable amongst the dowagers.'

My lady's brow vaulted while she contemplated that caution. She took her time; she was *not* to be hurried any more than she was to be *advised*. She lowered her chin, frowned, then tapped the table – a finger width of ash fell to the carpet, soon trodden beneath her foot.

'I am not a dowager. I earn my way.'

'You are a contrarian.'

She nodded, slightly and slowly. The gesture spoke of self-satisfaction; *more*, it demonstrated supercilious unconcern. Scarlett crossed her legs, lowered her brow and gazed at me under her lids.

'I am a woman.'

Queen Cleopatra, Empress Wu and Bloody Mary crowded into my mind, as did the eviscerations and the flames of the stake. My collar was becoming sore. I eased it with a finger.

She smiled. It was a smile that pulled straight her lips but did not crinkle her eyes. Dilated nostrils drew breath and she leaned back. The smouldering cigar was drawn into a glow with those lips. The roll of aromatic leaves was held up and back – cocked like a pirate's pistol or a chieftain's war feather. She was being *very* deliberate. Was I to slither beneath her contempt or was I to *rise* like a man? Cigar smoke was lifting behind her as she pointed at me with her long finger. Her boldness was turning into an exquisite insult. Even a peaceful man could not, should not, have restrained himself under such taunting. A red mist fell in front of me. In my eyes, her auburn hair seemed to blaze.

Without thought or word, I reached out a slap.

'There.'

She exploded and slapped me back.

Pah! The woman had no gratitude. The red mist was whisps of her red hair glowing. I had just saved the cigar from setting her head on fire.

Note: Concubine Wu eliminated her rivals to become Empress of China.

Scarlett & The Bright Colours

Women, say they, are better at colours than men.

'John, your consulting room needs redecoration. That embossed maroon paper is moody. It is patent that your patient patients, waiting in your waiting room, are depressed.'

'So am I, now.'

'Don't be petulant.'

'What must I agree to?

'Well, yellow would cheer it up, they need sun.'

'It has a north window. I cannot examine ladies next to the front window, even with muslin curtains.'

'Well, you could have them point to the place on a figurine; professional men of delicate disposition do that with ladies who need their help.'

'Engineers?'

'*Doctors,* John. Naples Yellow is brighter.'

'It would make them feel sick.'

'Give them an elixir.'

'Ah, Al-Iksir, the universal medicine? You are creeping into alchemy; they seek bright colours – gold from lead – mysticism. *I* am a man of science, Scarlett, and I do sometimes wonder at your predilection for the occult.'

'Newton was an alchemist; it had been quite normal knowledge. Shakespeare considered it to be part of an educated man's understanding. Why! Isaac had divided the very sunlight into colours. I am talking to you about colour, John.'

'My dear lady, do you allude to the philosopher's stone: black to purple? Mary the Jewess wrote about that in the fourth century – *she* was an alchemist.'

'*There,* you agree. Women know about colour. I know about colour. Now, ask a decorator to paper your room so we can all feel better.'

It was a pretty speech, but I was still feeling this was too much in the orbit of incantations and conjurations for a man of science like myself.

'Making the philosophers' stone has led some people to madness, Scarlett. There are rumours about the vermillion.'

'Which explains about that dimwit Sherlock; he has that colour in his bedroom rug. What rumours? Are you just trying to avoid the Naples yellow, John? Artists use it all the time.'

'Scarlett, having crushed gemstone or even beetles to make the paint for brushstrokes in a picture is not quite the same as having it all over the wall. Let me tell you, there are rumours about Napoleon – he slept in a room with green wallpaper and died. I think I will give the wallpaper idea a miss.

Scarlett & The Shame

Scarlett wore black for several week after her loss. It was after the news that her maternal paternal aunt had gone to her Maker, rather as had our dear queen.

'John I should have made time to see her more in these latter years, but I have been so busy. She was always there, always warm. Now she is cold. She is a spirit above me, still caring for me.'

Scarlett was well woven within the skeins of the ethereal. Her noesis, had qualities of some eternal power quite beyond a mortal man.

'Would it ease you to contact her through a medium perhaps?'

'I am a medium, John; I communicate with dark passages.' She tossed her chin. 'I have means of covert communication – a coven almost. I will set up a séance.'

I suspected that the dark passages were at those at the back of the ministry offices, and the coven was cast as convenient collegiate cover.

That evening, when the coal scented air had dimmed out the last vestiges of day, Scarlett, and I sat at a table in a small room at her club. The atmosphere inside was no less smoky than the

189

street, but more fragrant, joss sticks glowing at their tips. It was darkened by heavy velvet curtains and lightened by the reflection from Scarlett's face – spectral. At each side of her, stubs of candles flickered. Each had by the wick, in that well of hot wax, a small glowing pip of resin – a product of the poppy. The table was circular, normally used for intimate suppers by lady members with a desire for that sort of thing. In the middle was a crystal ball.

By this time Scarlett had absorbed some of the resin smoke and was murmuring in an elevated state. We all were commanded to set our hands on the table, fingers spread. We sat, silent but breathing wisps of the smoke for a long time, as Scarlett's murmuring rose and fell. Her sorority joined in the repetitive words; swaying left to right in harmony. Such muttering of a mantra could lift the mind to mountain tops of the ethereal. Slowly, she raised her hands to her face, thumbs touching but fingers angled as if in prayer.

Only two tall very thin candles remained. The light now was mostly in the mind. A glow formed above the glass ball: ectoplasm. It stretched up. Did I see it? Was it there or was it within my head? It seemed the shape of Scarlett but wizened –her aunt? The apparition was yellowy, willowy and billowy as if it were not really there, a trick of the light or more likely a murky miasma of mesmerism. We had all been brought to a state where our minds had flown high where clouds float and thoughts were as the whispers of the gods, leaving scepticism down low, in the gravel.

Hearts were beating, nerves were stretched, anticipation was building. Something was to happen. Something *had* to happen. A summer's day could feel so close, so tense that only a storm and the scissoring of the sky could relieve us of the tension. We *wanted* it to happen.

A choral voice, lower in register than Scarlett's, but as mellifluous, filled the smoky room as might a wraith floating on the zephyrs above the candles. The ladies had all parted their lips and were murmuring in unison. It was not that any one of them spoke, it was all of them; a creature constructed of all of them. They did not know that they spoke.

'Child, you are a forbidden creature.'

Scarlett's eyes, looking out at nothing but straight and unmoving, became red. The ladies shed tears. The light from the dwindling candles reflected in sheens from dampened lashes. Scarlett showed shame. Now she knew what she had only suspected.

'Child, you are barren, you are the product of a Devil's union. Your aunt is your mother, a woman whose devouring desires were devilish. The consequence of that cursed congress –

191

you will have no daughter and no son to perpetuate your gifts. You will be as fertile as a mare mule.'

Note: Victorians in Britain emphasised morality and the illegality of incest. In certain other European countries, it was not illegal.

Scarlett & The Tango

Women liked to upbraid men, Scarlett amongst them.

'John, you lack ambition.'

'What! I run a medical practice and I help your brother solve mysteries. More, I have been writing a biography of our exploits which I fully expect to be a classic of British writing *forever.*'

'Yes, but you have plateaued. You need a mountain to climb.'

Assailing mount Scarlett was ambition enough: high, mighty, and frosty. She *was* magnificent, though *and* mysterious.

'John, *I* will help you list points for your improvement. That moustache is too grey – use henna. Legs, too short – fillers in your shoes. Meek – try boxing. Music – leave Elgar to the brass band and try Borodin. Dancing – try . . . '

'Dear lady, you go too far. My dignity would be ruined if the henna were to drip on my shirt.'

'Dancing then. Smoking in a chair with that idle brother of mine is so dreary.'

Comfortable it was, but active it was not, I had to admit.

'Perhaps I could take you for a walk, Scarlett.'

'John, would you like to take me dancing?'

I was stricken. Gentlemen of my stamp do not dance.

'Dancing goes on at the common music hall.'

'*Feeble!* There is a dance in Paris just now that will liven you up. It is rather exotic; those hot-blooded Latin Americans get awfully close together.'

I felt warm, and not a little confused.

'The French, well, you know how the French behave, do it in darkened dance halls. Their parents are scandalised.'

There is something about an invitation from a lady to partake in bodily activity that would take a sterner man than me to resist.

-   -   -

Scarlett towed me into the dancehall much as she would a prize bull: by the nose. It was a fragrant darkness, lit only around the glow of red lamps on small tables. As I watched them, the dancers stepped and turned to the strange pulsing music of a wheezy band. They seemed to be submerged in a tide of irresistible emotion. Women, with their eyes closed, leaned their heads on chaps with slicked hair. They both transcended. I drew breath. Just then a lady, wearing black stockings took it into herself to swing one leg across the other. The movement would have caused my mother to gasp. I confessed that it quite took my eye; in fact, rather more of me than I felt comfortable relating. Scarlett noticed that and gave me a swift but wicked grin, then pulled me away to a table. We took with us large glasses of heavy red wine. Her own red dress, slashed to the thigh, swished as she walked in a way that…

Any reserve I still reserved was not preserved. There were ladies in spectacular dresses: bright red with flared skirts and shoes resembling stilts. One girl moved her leg to show a split that I tried not to look at. The lady in question had no trouble looking me and she did not pull in that split. I flattered myself that she might have been willing to dance. I just *had* to learn how.

Just then a sleazy fellow tipped his head to Scarlett, and she rose. Within moments, she was swirling like a fish in hot water, or a paid madam.

I had to learn the tango for more reasons than Scarlett, perhaps.

Note: In 1880, the dance: Tango Salon came to London from Buenos Aries, via Paris. It is a polite, skilled, elegant and erotic dance whose balletic difficulty engages the mind as well as the eye.

Author

L Charles Stribling

Qualifying early as an engineer had provided a working life rich in travel: Ecuador, Africa, America, Europe and Thailand.

In Britain, for many years he managed the design and construction of science buildings.

His other books are set in medieval Italy where he had property.

CPSIA information can be obtained
at www.ICGtesting.com
Printed in the USA
BVHW052306020323
659480BV00009B/1001

9 781804 240366